# A START IN LIFE

# DEDICATION

To Laure.

Let the brilliant mind that gave me the subject of this Scene have the honor of it.

Her brother,
De Balzac

# CONTENTS

# CHAPTER I

## THAT WHICH WAS LACKING TO
## PIERROTIN'S HAPPINESS

Railroads, in a future not far distant, must force certain industries to disappear forever, and modify several others, more especially those relating to the different modes of transportation in use around Paris. Therefore the persons and things which are the elements of this Scene will soon give to it the character of an archaeological work. Our nephews ought to be enchanted to learn the social material of an epoch which they will call the "olden time." The picturesque "coucous" which stood on the Place de la Concorde, encumbering the Cours-la-Reine,—coucous which had flourished for a century, and were still numerous in 1830, scarcely exist in 1842, unless on the occasion of some attractive suburban solemnity, like that of the Grandes Eaux of Versailles. In 1820, the various celebrated places called the "Environs of Paris" did not all possess a regular stage-coach service.

Nevertheless, the Touchards, father and son, had acquired a monopoly of travel and transportation to all the populous towns within a radius of forty-five miles; and their enterprise constituted a fine establishment in the rue du Faubourg-Saint-Denis. In spite of their long-standing rights, in spite, too, of their efforts, their capital, and all the advantages of a powerful centralization, the Touchard coaches ("messageries") found terrible competition in the coucou for all points with a circumference of fifteen or twenty miles. The passion of the Parisian for the country is such that local enterprise could successfully compete with the Lesser Stage company,—Petites Messageries, the name given to the Touchard enterprise to distinguish it from that of the Grandes Messageries of the rue Montmartre. At the time of which we write, the Touchard success was stimulating speculators. For every small locality in the neighborhood of Paris there sprang up schemes of beautiful, rapid, and commodious vehicles, departing and arriving in Paris at fixed hours, which produced, naturally, a fierce competition. Beaten on the long distances of twelve to eighteen miles, the coucou came down to shorter trips, and so lived on for several years. At last, however, it succumbed to omnibuses, which demonstrated the possibility of carrying eighteen persons in a vehicle drawn by two horses. To-day the coucous—if by chance any of those birds of ponderous flight still linger in the second-hand carriage-shops— might be made, as to its structure and arrangement, the subject of learned researches comparable to those of Cuvier on the animals discovered in the chalk pits of Montmartre.

These petty enterprises, which had struggled since 1822 against the Touchards, usually found a strong foothold in the good-will and sympathy of the inhabitants of the districts which they served. The person undertaking the business as proprietor and conductor was nearly always an inn-keeper along the route, to whom the beings, things, and interests with which he had to do were all familiar. He could execute commissions intelligently; he never asked as much for his little stages, and therefore obtained more custom than the Touchard coaches. He managed to elude the necessity of a custom-house permit. If need were, he was willing to infringe the law as to the number of passengers he might carry. In short, he possessed the affection of the masses; and thus it happened that whenever a rival came upon the same route, if his days for running were not the same as those of the coucou, travellers would put off their journey to make it with their long-tried coachman, although his vehicle and his horses might be in a far from reassuring condition.

One of the lines which the Touchards, father and son, endeavored to monopolize, and the one most stoutly disputed (as indeed it still is), is that of Paris to Beaumont-sur-Oise,—a line extremely profitable, for three rival enterprises worked it in 1822. In vain the Touchards lowered their price; in vain they constructed better coaches and started oftener. Competition still continued, so productive is a line on which are little towns like Saint-Denis and Saint-Brice, and villages like Pierrefitte, Groslay, Ecouen, Poncelles, Moisselles, Monsoult, Maffliers, Franconville, Presles, Nointel, Nerville, etc. The Touchard coaches finally extended their route to Chambly; but competition followed. To-day the Toulouse, a rival enterprise, goes as far as Beauvais.

Along this route, which is that toward England, there lies a road which turns off at a place well-named, in view of its topography, The Cave, and leads through a most delightful valley in the basin of the Oise to the little town of Isle-Adam, doubly celebrated as the cradle of the family, now extinct, of Isle-Adam, and also as the former residence of the Bourbon-Contis. Isle-Adam is a little town flanked by two large villages, Nogent and Parmain, both remarkable for splendid quarries, which have furnished material for many of the finest buildings in modern Paris and in foreign lands,—for the base and capital of the columns of the Brussels theatre are of Nogent stone. Though remarkable for its beautiful sites, for the famous chateaux which princes, monks, and designers have built, such as Cassan, Stors, Le Val, Nointel, Persan, etc., this region had escaped competition in 1822, and was reached by two coaches only, working more or less in harmony.

This exception to the rule of rivalry was founded on reasons that are easy to understand. From the Cave, the point on the route to England where a paved road (due to the luxury of the Princes of Conti) turned off to Isle-Adam, the distance is six miles. No speculating enterprise would make such a detour, for Isle-Adam was the terminus of the road, which did not go beyond it. Of late years, another road has been made between the valley of Montmorency and the valley of the Oise; but in

1822 the only road which led to Isle-Adam was the paved highway of the Princes of Conti. Pierrotin and his colleague reigned, therefore, from Paris to Isle-Adam, beloved by every one along the way. Pierrotin's vehicle, together with that of his comrade, and Pierrotin himself, were so well known that even the inhabitants on the main road as far as the Cave were in the habit of using them; for there was always better chance of a seat to be had than in the Beaumont coaches, which were almost always full. Pierrotin and his competitor were on the best of terms. When the former started from Isle-Adam, the latter was returning from Paris, and vice versa.

It is unnecessary to speak of the rival. Pierrotin possessed the sympathies of his region; besides, he is the only one of the two who appears in this veracious narrative. Let it suffice you to know that the two coach proprietors lived under a good understanding, rivalled each other loyally, and obtained customers by honorable proceedings. In Paris they used, for economy's sake, the same yard, hotel, and stable, the same coach-house, office, and clerk. This detail is alone sufficient to show that Pierrotin and his competitor were, as the popular saying is, "good dough." The hotel at which they put up in Paris, at the corner of the rue d'Enghien, is still there, and is called the "Lion d'Argent." The proprietor of the establishment, which from time immemorial had lodged coachmen and coaches, drove himself for the great company of Daumartin, which was so firmly established that its neighbors, the Touchards, whose place of business was directly opposite, never dreamed of starting a rival coach on the Daumartin line.

Though the departures for Isle-Adam professed to take place at a fixed hour, Pierrotin and his co-rival practised an indulgence in that respect which won for them the grateful affection of the country-people, and also violent remonstrances on the part of strangers accustomed to the regularity of the great lines of public conveyances. But the two conductors of these vehicles, which were half diligence, half coucou, were invariably defended by their regular customers. The afternoon departure at four o'clock usually lagged on till half-past, while that of the morning, fixed for eight o'clock, was seldom known to take place before nine. In this respect, however, the system was elastic. In summer, that golden period for the coaching business, the rule of departure, rigorous toward strangers, was often relaxed for country customers. This method not infrequently enabled Pierrotin to pocket two fares for one place, if a countryman came early and wanted a seat already booked and paid for by some "bird of passage" who was, unluckily for himself, a little late. Such elasticity will certainly not commend itself to purists in morality; but Pierrotin and his colleague justified it on the varied grounds of "hard times," of their losses during the winter months, of the necessity of soon getting better coaches, and of the duty of keeping exactly to the rules written on the tariff, copies of which were, however, never shown, unless some chance traveller was obstinate enough to demand it.

Pierrotin, a man about forty years of age, was already the father of a family. Released from the cavalry on the great disbandment of 1815, the worthy fellow had succeeded his father, who for many years had driven a coucou of capricious flight between Paris and Isle-Adam. Having married the daughter of a small inn-keeper, he enlarged his business, made it a regular service, and became noted for his intelligence and a certain military precision. Active and decided in his ways, Pierrotin (the name seems to have been a sobriquet) contrived to give, by the vivacity of his countenance, an expression of sly shrewdness to his ruddy and weather-stained visage which suggested wit. He was not without that facility of speech which is acquired chiefly through "seeing life" and other countries. His voice, by dint of talking to his horses and shouting "Gare!" was rough; but he managed to tone it down with the bourgeois. His clothing, like that of all coachmen of the second class, consisted of stout boots, heavy with nails, made at Isle-Adam, trousers of bottle-green velveteen, waistcoat of the same, over which he wore, while exercising his functions, a blue blouse, ornamented on the collar, shoulder-straps and cuffs, with many-colored embroidery. A cap with a visor covered his head. His military career had left in Pierrotin's manners and customs a great respect for all social superiority, and a habit of obedience to persons of the upper classes; and though he never willingly mingled with the lesser bourgeoisie, he always respected women in whatever station of life they belonged. Nevertheless, by dint of "trundling the world,"—one of his own expressions,—he had come to look upon those he conveyed as so many walking parcels, who required less care than the inanimate ones,—the essential object of a coaching business.

Warned by the general movement which, since the Peace, was revolutionizing his calling, Pierrotin would not allow himself to be outdone by the progress of new lights. Since the beginning of the summer season he had talked much of a certain large coach, ordered from Farry, Breilmann, and Company, the best makers of diligences,—a purchase necessitated by an increasing influx of travellers. Pierrotin's present establishment consisted of two vehicles. One, which served in winter, and the only one he reported to the tax-gatherer, was the coucou which he inherited from his father. The rounded flanks of this vehicle allowed him to put six travellers on two seats, of metallic hardness in spite of the yellow Utrecht velvet with which they were covered. These seats were separated by a wooden bar inserted in the sides of the carriage at the height of the travellers' shoulders, which could be placed or removed at will. This bar, specially covered with velvet (Pierrotin called it "a back"), was the despair of the passengers, from the great difficulty they found in placing and removing it. If the "back" was difficult and even painful to handle, that was nothing to the suffering caused to the omoplates when the bar was in place. But when it was left to lie loose across the coach, it made both ingress and egress extremely perilous, especially to women.

Though each seat of this vehicle, with rounded sides like those of a pregnant woman, could rightfully carry only three passengers, it was not uncommon to see eight persons on the two seats jammed together like herrings in a barrel. Pierrotin declared that the travellers were far more comfortable in a solid, immovable mass; whereas when only three were on a seat they banged each other perpetually, and ran much risk of injuring their hats against the roof by the violent jolting of the roads. In front of the vehicle was a wooden bench where Pierrotin sat, on which three travellers could perch; when there, they went, as everybody knows, by the name of "rabbits." On certain trips Pierrotin placed four rabbits on the bench, and sat himself at the side, on a sort of box placed below the body of the coach as a foot-rest for the rabbits, which was always full of straw, or of packages that feared no damage. The body of this particular coucou was painted yellow, embellished along the top with a band of barber's blue, on which could be read, on the sides, in silvery white letters, "Isle-Adam, Paris," and across the back, "Line to Isle-Adam."

Our descendants will be mightily mistaken if they fancy that thirteen persons including Pierrotin were all that this vehicle could carry. On great occasions it could take three more in a square compartment covered with an awning, where the trunks, cases, and packages were piled; but the prudent Pierrotin only allowed his regular customers to sit there, and even they were not allowed to get in until at some distance beyond the "barriere." The occupants of the "hen-roost" (the name given by conductors to this section of their vehicles) were made to get down outside of every village or town where there was a post of gendarmerie; the overloading forbidden by law, "for the safety of passengers," being too obvious to allow the gendarme on duty—always a friend to Pierrotin—to avoid the necessity of reporting this flagrant violation of the ordinances. Thus on certain Saturday nights and Monday mornings, Pierrotin's coucou "trundled" fifteen travellers; but on such occasions, in order to drag it along, he gave his stout old horse, called Rougeot, a mate in the person of a little beast no bigger than a pony, about whose merits he had much to say. This little horse was a mare named Bichette; she ate little, she was spirited, she was indefatigable, she was worth her weight in gold.

"My wife wouldn't give her for that fat lazybones of a Rougeot!" cried Pierrotin, when some traveller would joke him about his epitome of a horse.

The difference between this vehicle and the other consisted chiefly in the fact that the other was on four wheels. This coach, of comical construction, called the "four-wheel-coach," held seventeen travellers, though it was bound not to carry more than fourteen. It rumbled so noisily that the inhabitants of Isle-Adam frequently said, "Here comes Pierrotin!" when he was scarcely out of the forest which crowns the slope of the valley. It was divided into two lobes, so to speak: one, called the "interior," contained six passengers on two seats; the other, a sort of cabriolet constructed in front, was called the "coupe." This coupe was closed in with very inconvenient and fantastic glass sashes, a description of which would take too much space to allow of its being given here. The four-wheeled coach was surmounted by a hooded "imperial," into which Pierrotin managed to poke six passengers; this space was inclosed by leather curtains. Pierrotin himself sat on an almost invisible seat perched just below the sashes of the coupe.

The master of the establishment paid the tax which was levied upon all public conveyances on his coucou only, which was rated to carry six persons; and he took out a special permit each time that he drove the four-wheeler. This may seem extraordinary in these days, but when the tax on vehicles was first imposed, it was done very timidly, and such deceptions were easily practised by the coach proprietors, always pleased to "faire la queue" (cheat of their dues) the government officials, to use the argot of their vocabulary. Gradually the greedy Treasury became severe; it forced all public conveyances not to roll unless they carried two certificates,—one showing that they had been weighed, the other that their taxes were duly paid. All things have their salad days, even the Treasury; and in 1822 those days still lasted. Often in summer, the "four-wheel-coach," and the coucou journeyed together, carrying between them thirty-two passengers, though Pierrotin was only paying a tax on six. On these specially lucky days the convoy started from the faubourg Saint-Denis at half-past four o'clock in the afternoon, and arrived gallantly at

Isle-Adam by ten at night. Proud of this service, which necessitated the hire of an extra horse, Pierrotin was wont to say:—

"We went at a fine pace!"

But in order to do the twenty-seven miles in five hours with his caravan, he was forced to omit certain stoppages along the road,—at Saint-Brice, Moisselles, and La Cave.

The hotel du Lion d'Argent occupies a piece of land which is very deep for its width. Though its frontage has only three or four windows on the faubourg Saint-Denis, the building extends back through a long court-yard, at the end of which are the stables, forming a large house standing close against the division wall of the adjoining property. The entrance is through a sort of passage-way beneath the floor of the second story, in which two or three coaches had room to stand. In 1822 the offices of all the lines of coaches which started from the Lion d'Argent were kept by the wife of the inn-keeper, who had as many books as there were lines. She received the fares, booked the passengers, and stowed away, good-naturedly, in her vast kitchen the various packages and parcels to be transported. Travellers were satisfied with this easy-going, patriarchal system. If they arrived too soon, they seated themselves beneath the hood of the huge kitchen chimney, or stood within the passage-way, or crossed to the Cafe de l'Echiquier, which forms the corner of the street so named.

In the early days of the autumn of 1822, on a Saturday morning, Pierrotin was standing, with his hands thrust into his pockets through the apertures of his blouse, beneath the porte-cochere of the Lion d'Argent, whence he could see, diagonally, the kitchen of the inn, and through the long court-yard to the stables, which were defined in black at the end of it. Daumartin's diligence had just started, plunging heavily after those of the Touchards. It was past eight o'clock. Under the enormous porch or passage, above which could be read on a long sign, "Hotel du Lion d'Argent," stood the stablemen and porters of the coaching-lines watching the lively start of the vehicles which deceives so many travellers, making them believe that the horses will be kept to that vigorous gait.

"Shall I harness up, master?" asked Pierrotin's hostler, when there was nothing more to be seen along the road.

"It is a quarter-past eight, and I don't see any travellers," replied Pierrotin. "Where have they poked themselves? Yes, harness up all the same. And there are no parcels either! Twenty good Gods! a fine day like this, and I've only four booked! A pretty state of things for a Saturday! It is always the same when you want money! A dog's life, and a dog's business!"

"If you had more, where would you put them? There's nothing left but the cabriolet," said the hostler, intending to soothe Pierrotin.

"You forget the new coach!" cried Pierrotin.

"Have you really got it?" asked the man, laughing, and showing a set of teeth as white and broad as almonds.

"You old good-for-nothing! It starts to-morrow, I tell you; and I want at least eighteen passengers for it."

"Ha, ha! a fine affair; it'll warm up the road," said the hostler.

"A coach like that which runs to Beaumont, hey? Flaming! painted red and gold to make Touchard burst with envy! It takes three horses! I have bought a mate for Rougeot, and Bichette will go finely in unicorn. Come, harness up!" added Pierrotin, glancing out towards the street, and stuffing the tobacco into his clay pipe. "I see a lady and lad over there with packages under their arms; they are coming to the Lion d'Argent, for they've turned a deaf ear to the coucous. Tiens, tiens! seems to me I know that lady for an old customer."

"You've often started empty, and arrived full," said his porter, still by way of consolation.

"But no parcels! Twenty good Gods! What a fate!"

And Pierrotin sat down on one of the huge stone posts which protected the walls of the building from the wheels of the coaches; but he did so with an anxious, reflective air that was not habitual with him.

This conversation, apparently insignificant, had stirred up cruel anxieties which were slumbering in his breast. What could there be to trouble the heart of Pierrotin in a fine new coach? To shine upon "the road," to rival the Touchards, to magnify his own line, to carry passengers who would compliment him on the conveniences due to the progress of coach-building, instead of having to listen to perpetual complaints of his "sabots" (tires of enormous width),—such was Pierrotin's laudable ambition; but, carried away with the desire to outstrip his comrade on the line, hoping that the latter might some day retire and leave to him alone the transportation to Isle-Adam, he had gone too far. The coach was indeed ordered from Barry, Breilmann, and Company, coach-builders, who had just substituted square English springs for those called "swan-necks," and other old-fashioned French contrivances. But these hard and distrustful manufacturers would only deliver over the diligence in return for coin. Not particularly pleased to build a vehicle which would be difficult to sell if it remained upon their hands, these long-headed dealers declined to undertake it at all until Pierrotin had made a preliminary payment of two thousand francs. To satisfy this precautionary demand, Pierrotin had exhausted all his resources and all his credit. His wife, his father-in-law, and his friends had bled. This superb diligence he had been to see the evening before at the painter's; all it needed now was to be set a-rolling, but to make it roll, payment in full must, alas! be made.

Now, a thousand francs were lacking to Pierrotin, and where to get them he did not know. He was in debt to the master of the Lion d'Argent; he was in danger of his losing his two thousand francs already paid to the coach-builder, not counting five hundred for the mate to Rougeot, and three hundred for new harnesses, on which he had a three-months' credit. Driven by the fury of despair and the madness of vanity, he had just openly declared that the new coach was to start on the morrow. By offering fifteen hundred francs, instead of the two thousand five hundred still due, he was in hopes that the softened carriage-builders would give him his coach. But after a few moments' meditation, his feelings led him to cry out aloud:—

"No! they're dogs! harpies! Suppose I appeal to Monsieur Moreau, the steward at Presles? he is such a kind man," thought Pierrotin, struck with a new idea. "Perhaps he would take my note for six months."

At this moment a footman in livery, carrying a leather portmanteau and coming from the Touchard establishment, where he had gone too late to secure places as far as Chambly, came up and said:—

"Are you Pierrotin?"

"Say on," replied Pierrotin.

"If you would wait a quarter of an hour, you could take my master. If not, I'll carry back the portmanteau and try to find some other conveyance."

"I'll wait two, three quarters, and throw a little in besides, my lad," said Pierrotin, eyeing the pretty leather trunk, well buckled, and bearing a brass plate with a coat of arms.

"Very good; then take this," said the valet, ridding his shoulder of the trunk, which Pierrotin lifted, weighed, and examined.

"Here," he said to his porter, "wrap it up carefully in soft hay and put it in the boot. There's no name upon it," he added.

"Monseigneur's arms are there," replied the valet.

"Monseigneur! Come and take a glass," said Pierrotin, nodding toward the Cafe de l'Echiquier, whither he conducted the valet. "Waiter, two absinthes!" he said, as he entered. "Who is your master? and where is he going? I have never seen you before," said Pierrotin to the valet as they touched glasses.

"There's a good reason for that," said the footman. "My master only goes into your parts about once a year, and then in his own carriage. He prefers the valley d'Orge, where he has the most beautiful park in the neighborhood of Paris, a perfect Versailles, a family estate of which he bears the name. Don't you know Monsieur Moreau?"

"The steward of Presles?"

"Yes. Monsieur le Comte is going down to spend a couple of days with him."

"Ha! then I'm to carry Monsieur le Comte de Serizy!" cried the coach-proprietor.

"Yes, my land, neither more nor less. But listen! here's a special order. If you have any of the country neighbors in your coach you are not to call him Monsieur le comte; he wants to travel 'en cognito,' and told me to be sure to say he would pay a handsome pourboire if he was not recognized."

"So! Has this secret journey anything to do with the affair which Pere Leger, the farmer at the Moulineaux, came to Paris the other day to settle?"

"I don't know," replied the valet, "but the fat's in the fire. Last night I was sent to the stable to order the Daumont carriage to be ready to go to Presles at seven this morning. But when seven o'clock came, Monsieur le comte countermanded it. Augustin, his valet de chambre, attributes the change to the visit of a lady who called last night, and again this morning,—he thought she came from the country."

"Could she have told him anything against Monsieur Moreau?—the best of men, the most honest of men, a king of men, hey! He might have made a deal more than he has out of his position, if he'd chosen; I can tell you that."

"Then he was foolish," answered the valet, sententiously.

"Is Monsieur le Serizy going to live at Presles at last?" asked Pierrotin; "for you know they have just repaired and refurnished the chateau. Do you think it is true he has already spent two hundred thousand francs upon it?"

"If you or I had half what he has spent upon it, you and I would be rich bourgeois. If Madame la comtesse goes there—ha! I tell you what! no more ease and comfort for the Moreaus," said the valet, with an air of mystery.

"He's a worthy man, Monsieur Moreau," remarked Pierrotin, thinking of the thousand francs he wanted to get from the steward. "He is a man who makes others work, but he doesn't cheapen what they do; and he gets all he can out of the land—for his master. Honest man! He often comes to Paris and gives me a good fee: he has lots of errands for me to do in Paris; sometimes three or four packages a day,—either from monsieur or madame. My bill for cartage alone comes to fifty francs a month, more or less. If madame does set up to be somebody, she's fond of her children; and it is I who fetch them from school and take them back; and each time she gives me five francs,—a real great lady couldn't do better than that. And every time I have any one in the coach belonging to them or going to see them, I'm allowed to drive up to the chateau,—that's all right, isn't it?"

"They say Monsieur Moreau wasn't worth three thousand francs when Monsieur le comte made him steward of Presles," said the valet.

"Well, since 1806, there's seventeen years, and the man ought to have made something at any rate."

"True," said the valet, nodding. "Anyway, masters are very annoying; and I hope, for Moreau's sake, that he has made butter for his bread."

"I have often been to your house in the rue de la Chaussee d'Antin to carry baskets of game," said Pierrotin, "but I've never had the advantage, so far of seeing either monsieur or madame."

"Monsieur le comte is a good man," said the footman, confidentially. "But if he insists on your helping to keep up his cognito there's something in the wind. At any rate, so we think at the house; or else, why should he countermand the Daumont,—why travel in a coucou? A peer of France might afford to hire a cabriolet to himself, one would think."

"A cabriolet would cost him forty francs to go there and back; for let me tell you, if you don't know it, that road was only made for squirrels,— up-hill and down, down-hill and up!" said Pierrotin. "Peer of France or bourgeois, they are all looking after the main chance, and saving their money. If this journey concerns Monsieur Moreau, faith, I'd be sorry any harm should come to him! Twenty good Gods! hadn't I better find some way of warning him?—for he's a truly good man, a kind man, a king of men, hey!"

"Pooh! Monsieur le comte thinks everything of Monsieur Moreau," replied the valet. "But let me give you a bit of good advice. Every man for himself in this world. We have enough to do to take care of ourselves. Do what Monsieur le comte asks you to do, and all the more because there's no trifling with him. Besides, to tell the truth, the count is generous. If you oblige him so far," said the valet, pointing half-way down his little finger, "he'll send you on as far as that," stretching out his arm to its full length.

This wise reflection, and the action that enforced it, had the effect, coming from a man who stood as high as second valet to the Comte de Serizy, of cooling the ardor of Pierrotin for the steward of Presles.

"Well, adieu, Monsieur Pierrotin," said the valet.

A glance rapidly cast on the life of the Comte de Serizy, and on that of his steward, is here necessary in order to fully understand the little drama now about to take place in Pierrotin's vehicle.

# CHAPTER II

## THE STEWARD IN DANGER

Monsieur Huguet de Serisy descends in a direct line from the famous president Huguet, ennobled under Francois I.

This family bears: party per pale or and sable, an orle counterchanged and two lozenges counterchanged, with: "i, semper melius eris,"—a motto which, together with the two distaffs taken as supporters, proves the modesty of the burgher families in the days when the Orders held their allotted places in the State; and the naivete of our ancient customs by the pun on "eris," which word, combined with the "i" at the beginning and the final "s" in "melius," forms the name (Serisy) of the estate from which the family take their title.

The father of the present count was president of a parliament before the Revolution. He himself a councillor of State at the Grand Council of 1787, when he was only twenty-two years of age, was even then distinguished for his admirable memoranda on delicate diplomatic matters. He did not emigrate during the Revolution, and spent that period on his estate of Serizy near Arpajon, where the respect in which his father was held protected him from all danger. After spending several years in taking care of the old president, who died in 1794, he was elected about that time to the Council of the Five Hundred, and accepted those legislative functions to divert his mind from his grief. After the 18th Brumaire, Monsieur de Serizy became, like so many other of the old parliamentary families, an object of the First Consul's blandishment. He was appointed to the Council of State, and received one of the most disorganized departments of the government to reconstruct. This scion of an old historical family proved to be a very active wheel in the grand and magnificent organization which we owe to Napoleon.

The councillor of State was soon called from his particular administration to a ministry. Created count and senator by the Emperor, he was made proconsul to two kingdoms in succession. In 1806, when forty years of age, he married the sister of the ci-devant Marquis de Ronquerolles, the widow at twenty of Gaubert, one of the most illustrious of the Republican generals, who left her his whole property. This marriage, a suitable one in point of rank, doubled the already considerable fortune of the Comte de Serizy, who became through his wife the brother-in-law of the ci-devant Marquis de Rouvre, made count and chamberlain by the Emperor.

In 1814, weary with constant toil, the Comte de Serizy, whose shattered health required rest, resigned all his posts, left the department at the head of which the Emperor had placed him, and came to Paris, where Napoleon was compelled by the evidence of his eyes to admit that the count's illness was a valid excuse, though at first that *unfatiguable* master, who gave no heed to the fatigue of others, was disposed to consider Monsieur de Serizy's action as a defection. Though the senator was never in disgrace, he was supposed to have reason to complain of Napoleon. Consequently, when the Bourbons returned, Louis XVIII., whom Monsieur de Serizy held to be his legitimate sovereign, treated the senator, now a peer of France, with the utmost confidence, placed him in charge of his private affairs, and appointed him one of his cabinet ministers. On the 20th of March, Monsieur de Serizy did not go to Ghent. He informed Napoleon that he remained faithful to the house of Bourbon; would not accept his peerage during the Hundred Days, and passed that period on his estate at Serizy.

After the second fall of the Emperor, he became once more a privy-councillor, was appointed vice-president of the Council of State, and liquidator, on behalf of France, of claims and indemnities demanded by foreign powers. Without personal assumption, without ambition even, he possessed great influence in public affairs. Nothing of importance was done without consulting him; but he never went to court, and was seldom seen in his own salons. This noble life, devoting itself from its very beginning to work, had ended by becoming a life of incessant toil. The count rose at all seasons by four o'clock in the morning, and worked till mid-day, attended to his functions as peer of France and vice-president of the Council of State in the afternoons, and went to bed at nine o'clock. In recognition of such labor, the King had made him a knight of his various Orders. Monsieur de Serizy had long worn the grand cross of the Legion of honor; he also had the orders of the Golden Fleece, of Saint-Andrew of Russia, that of the Prussian Eagle, and nearly all the lesser Orders of the courts of Europe. No man was less obvious, or more useful in the political world than he. It is easy to understand that the world's honor, the fuss and feathers of public favor, the glories of success were indifferent to a man of this stamp; but no one, unless a priest, ever comes to life of this kind without some serious underlying reason. His conduct had its cause, and a cruel one.

In love with his wife before he married her, this passion had lasted through all the secret unhappiness of his marriage with a widow,—a woman mistress of herself before as well as after her second marriage, and who used her liberty all the more freely because her husband treated her with the indulgence of a mother for a spoilt child. His constant toil served him as shield and buckler against pangs of heart which he silenced with the care that diplomatists give to the keeping of secrets. He knew, moreover, how ridiculous was jealousy in the eyes of a society that would never have believed in the conjugal passion of an old statesman. How happened it that from the earliest days of his marriage his wife so fascinated him? Why did he suffer without resistance? How was it that he dared not resist? Why did he let the years go by and still hope on? By what means did this young and pretty and clever woman hold him in bondage?

The answer to all these questions would require a long history, which would injure our present tale. Let us only remark here that the constant toil and grief of the count had unfortunately contributed not a little to deprive him of personal advantages very necessary to a man who attempts to struggle against dangerous comparisons. In fact, the most cruel of the count's secret sorrows was that of causing repugnance to his wife by a malady of the skin resulting solely from excessive labor. Kind, and always considerate of the countess, he allowed her to be mistress of herself and her home. She received all Paris; she went into the country; she returned from it precisely as though she were still a widow. He took care of her fortune and supplied her luxury as a steward might have done. The countess had the utmost respect for her husband. She even admired his turn of mind; she knew how to make him happy by approbation; she could do what she pleased with him by simply going to his study and talking for an hour with him. Like the great seigneurs of the olden time, the count protected his wife so loyally that a single word of disrespect said of her would have been to him an unpardonable injury. The world admired him for this; and Madame de Serizy owed much to it. Any other woman, even though she came of a family as distinguished as the Ronquerolles, might have found herself degraded in public opinion. The countess was ungrateful, but she mingled a charm with her ingratitude. From time to time she shed a balm upon the wounds of her husband's heart.

Let us now explain the meaning of this sudden journey, and the incognito maintained by a minister of State.

A rich farmer of Beaumont-sur-Oise, named Leger, leased and cultivated a farm, the fields of which projected into and greatly injured the magnificent estate of the Comte de Serizy, called Presles. This farm belonged to a burgher of Beaumont-sur-Oise, named Margueron. The lease made to Leger in 1799, at a time when the great advance of agriculture was not foreseen, was about to expire, and the owner of the farm refused all offers from Leger to renew the lease. For some time past, Monsieur de Serizy, wishing to rid himself of the annoyances and petty disputes caused by the inclosure of these fields within his land, had desired to buy the farm, having heard that Monsieur Margueron's chief ambition was to have his only son, then a mere tax-gatherer, made special collector of finances at Beaumont. The farmer, who knew he could sell the fields piecemeal to the count at a high price, was ready to pay Margueron even more than he expected from the count.

Thus matters stood when, two days earlier than that of which we write, Monsieur de Serizy, anxious to end the matter, sent for his notary, Alexandre Crottat, and his lawyer, Derville, to examine into all the circumstances of the affair. Though Derville and Crottat threw some doubt on the zeal of the count's steward (a disturbing letter from whom had led to the consultation), Monsieur de Serizy defended Moreau, who, he said, had served him faithfully for seventeen years.

"Very well!" said Derville, "then I advise your Excellency to go to Presles yourself, and invite this Margueron to dinner. Crottat will send his head-clerk with a deed of sale drawn up, leaving only the necessary lines for description of property and titles in blank. Your Excellency should take with you part of the purchase money in a check on the Bank of France, not forgetting the appointment of the son to the collectorship. If you don't settle the thing at once that farm will slip through your fingers. You don't know, Monsieur le comte, the trickery of these peasants. Peasants against diplomat, and the diplomat succumbs."

Crottat agreed in this advice, which the count, if we may judge by the valet's statements to Pierrotin, had adopted. The preceding evening he had sent Moreau a line by the diligence to Beaumont, telling him to invite Margueron to dinner in order that they might then and there close the purchase of the farm of Moulineaux.

Before this matter came up, the count had already ordered the chateau of Presles to be restored and refurnished, and for the last year, Grindot, an architect then in fashion, was in the habit of making a weekly visit. So, while concluding his purchase of the farm, Monsieur de Serizy also intended to examine the work of restoration and the effect of the new furniture. He intended all this to be a surprise to his wife when he brought her to Presles, and with this idea in his mind, he had put some personal pride and self-love into the work. How came it therefore that the count, who intended in the evening to drive to Presles openly in his own carriage, should be starting early the next morning incognito in Pierrotin's coucou?

Here a few words on the life of the steward Moreau become indispensable.

Moreau, steward of the state of Presles, was the son of a provincial attorney who became during the Revolution syndic-attorney at Versailles. In that position, Moreau the father had been the means of almost saving both the lives and property of the Serizys, father and son. Citizen Moreau belonged to the Danton party; Robespierre, implacable in his hatreds, pursued him, discovered him, and finally had him executed at Versailles. Moreau the son, heir to the doctrines and friendships of his father, was concerned in one of the conspiracies which assailed the First Consul on his accession to power. At this crisis, Monsieur de Serizy, anxious to pay his debt of gratitude, enabled Moreau, lying under sentence of death, to make his escape; in 1804 he asked for his pardon, obtained it, offered him first a place in his government office, and finally took him as private secretary for his own affairs.

Some time after the marriage of his patron Moreau fell in love with the countess's waiting-woman and married her. To avoid the annoyances of the false position in which this marriage placed him (more than one example of which could be seen at the imperial court), Moreau asked the count to give him the management of the Presles estate, where his wife could play the lady in a country region, and neither of them would be made to suffer from wounded self-love. The count wanted a trustworthy man at Presles, for his wife preferred Serizy, an estate only fifteen miles from Paris. For three or four years Moreau had held the key of the count's affairs; he was intelligent, and before the Revolution he had studied law in his father's office; so Monsieur de Serizy granted his request.

"You can never advance in life," he said to Moreau, "for you have broken your neck; but you can be happy, and I will take care that you are so."

He gave Moreau a salary of three thousand francs and his residence in a charming lodge near the chateau, all the wood he needed from the timber that was cut on the estate, oats, hay, and straw for two horses, and a right to whatever he wanted of the produce of the gardens. A sub-prefect is not as well provided for.

During the first eight years of his stewardship, Moreau managed the estate conscientiously; he took an interest in it. The count, coming down now and then to examine the property, pass judgment on what had been done, and decide on new purchases, was struck with Moreau's evident loyalty, and showed his satisfaction by liberal gifts.

But after the birth of Moreau's third child, a daughter, he felt himself so securely settled in all his comforts at Presles that he ceased to attribute to Monsieur de Serizy those enormous advantages. About the year 1816, the steward, who until then had only taken what he needed for his own use from the estate, accepted a sum of twenty-five thousand francs from a wood-merchant as an inducement to lease to the latter, for twelve years, the cutting of all the timber. Moreau argued this: he could have no pension; he was the father of a family; the count really owed him that sum as a gift after ten years' management; already the legitimate possessor of sixty thousand francs in savings, if he added this sum to that, he could buy a farm worth a hundred and twenty-five thousand francs in Champagne, a township just above Isle-Adam, on the right bank of the Oise. Political events prevented both the count and the neighboring country-people from becoming aware of this investment, which was made in the name of Madame Moreau, who was understood to have inherited property from an aunt of her father.

As soon as the steward had tasted the delightful fruit of the possession of the property, he began, all the while maintaining toward the world an appearance of the utmost integrity, to lose no occasion of increasing his fortune clandestinely; the interests of his three children served as a poultice to the wounds of his honor. Nevertheless, we ought in justice to say that while he accepted casks of wine, and took care of himself in all the purchases that he made for the count, yet according to the terms of the Code he remained an honest man, and no proof could have been found to justify an accusation against him. According to the jurisprudence of the least thieving cook in Paris, he shared with the count in the profits due to his own capable management. This manner of swelling his fortune was simply a case of conscience, that was all. Alert, and thoroughly understanding the count's interests, Moreau watched for opportunities to make good purchases all the more eagerly, because he gained a larger percentage on them. Presles returned a revenue of seventy thousand francs net. It was a saying of the country-side for a circuit of thirty miles:—

"Monsieur de Serizy has a second self in Moreau."

Being a prudent man, Moreau invested yearly, after 1817, both his profits and his salary on the Grand Livre, piling up his heap with the utmost secrecy. He often refused proposals on the plea of want of money; and he played the poor man so successfully with the count that the latter gave him the means to send both his sons to the school Henri IV. At the present moment Moreau was worth one hundred and twenty thousand francs of capital invested in the Consolidated thirds, now paying five per cent, and quoted at eighty francs. These carefully hidden one hundred and twenty thousand francs, and his farm at Champagne, enlarged by subsequent purchases, amounted to a fortune of about two hundred and eighty thousand francs, giving him an income of some sixteen thousand.

Such was the position of the steward at the time when the Comte de Serizy desired to purchase the farm of Moulineaux,—the ownership of which was indispensable to his comfort. This farm consisted of ninety-six parcels of land bordering the estate of Presles, and frequently running into it, producing the most annoying discussions as to the trimming of hedges and ditches and the cutting of trees. Any other than a cabinet minister would probably have had scores of lawsuits on his hands. Pere Leger only wished to buy the property in order to sell to the count at a handsome advance. In order to secure the exorbitant sum on which his mind was set, the farmer had long endeavored to come to an understanding with Moreau. Impelled by circumstances, he had, only three days before this critical Sunday, had a talk with the steward in the open field, and proved to him clearly that he (Moreau) could make the count invest his money at two and a half per cent, and thus appear to serve his patron's interests, while he himself pocketed forty thousand francs which Leger offered him to bring about the transaction.

"I tell you what," said the steward to his wife, as he went to bed that night, "if I make fifty thousand francs out of the Moulineaux affair,—and I certainly shall, for the count will give me ten thousand as a fee,—we'll retire to Isle-Adam and live in the Pavillon de Nogent."

This "pavillon" was a charming place, originally built by the Prince de Conti for a mistress, and in it every convenience and luxury had been placed.

"That will suit me," said his wife. "The Dutchman who lives there has put it in good order, and now that he is obliged to return to India, he would probably let us have it for thirty thousand francs."

"We shall be close to Champagne," said Moreau. "I am in hopes of buying the farm and mill of Mours for a hundred thousand francs. That would give us ten thousand a year in rentals. Nogent is one of the most delightful residences in the valley; and we should still have an income of ten thousand from the Grand-Livre."

"But why don't you ask for the post of juge-de-paix at Isle-Adam? That would give us influence, and fifteen hundred a year salary."

"Well, I did think of it."

With these plans in mind, Moreau, as soon as he heard from the count that he was coming to Presles, and wished him to invite Margueron to dinner on Saturday, sent off an express to the count's head-valet, inclosing a letter to his master, which the messenger failed to deliver before Monsieur de Serizy retired at his usually early hour. Augustin, however, placed it, according to custom in such cases, on his master's desk. In this letter Moreau begged the count not to trouble himself to come down, but to trust entirely to him. He added that Margueron was no longer willing to sell the whole in one block, and talked of cutting the farm up into a number of smaller lots. It was necessary to circumvent this plan, and perhaps, added Moreau, it might be best to employ a third party to make the purchase.

Everybody has enemies in this life. Now the steward and his wife had wounded the feelings of a retired army officer, Monsieur de Reybert, and his wife, who were living near Presles. From speeches like pin-pricks, matters had advanced to dagger-thrusts. Monsieur de Reybert breathed vengeance. He was determined to make Moreau lose his situation and gain it himself. The two ideas were twins. Thus the proceedings of the steward, spied upon for two years, were no secret to Reybert. The same conveyance that took Moreau's letter to the count conveyed Madame de Reybert, whom her husband despatched to Paris. There she asked with such earnestness to see the count that although she was sent away at nine o'clock, he having then gone to bed, she was ushered into his study the next morning at seven.

"Monsieur," she said to the cabinet-minister, "we are incapable, my husband and I, of writing anonymous letters, therefore I have come to see you in person. I am Madame de Reybert, nee de Corroy. My husband is a retired officer, with a pension of six hundred francs, and we live at Presles, where your steward has offered us insult after insult, although we are persons of good station. Monsieur de Reybert, who is not an intriguing man, far from it, is a captain of artillery, retired in 1816, having served twenty years,—always at a distance from the Emperor, Monsieur le comte. You know of course how difficult it is for soldiers who are not under the eye of their master to obtain promotion,—not counting that the integrity and frankness of Monsieur de Reybert were displeasing to his superiors. My husband has watched your steward for the last three years, being aware of his dishonesty and intending to have him lose his place. We are, as you see, quite frank with you. Moreau has made us his enemies, and we have watched him. I have come to tell you that you are being tricked in the purchase of the Moulineaux farm. They mean to get an extra hundred thousand francs out of you, which are to be divided between the notary, the farmer Leger, and Moreau. You have written Moreau to invite Margueron, and you are going to Presles to-day; but Margueron will be ill, and Leger is so certain of buying the farm that he is now in Paris to draw the money. If we have enlightened you as to what is going on, and if you want an upright steward you will take my husband; though noble, he will serve you as he has served the State. Your steward has made a fortune of two hundred and fifty thousand francs out of his place; he is not to be pitied therefore."

The count thanked Madame de Reybert coldly, bestowing upon her the holy-water of courts, for he despised backbiting; but for all that, he remembered Derville's doubts, and felt inwardly shaken. Just then he saw his steward's letter and read it. In its assurances of devotion and its respectful reproaches for the distrust implied in wishing to negotiate the purchase for himself, he read the truth.

"Corruption has come to him with fortune,—as it always does!" he said to himself.

The count then made several inquiries of Madame de Reybert, less to obtain information than to gain time to observe her; and he wrote a short note to his notary telling him not to send his head-clerk to Presles as requested, but to come there himself in time for dinner.

"Though Monsieur le comte," said Madame de Reybert in conclusion, "may have judged me unfavorably for the step I have taken unknown to my husband, he ought to be convinced that we have obtained this information about his steward in a natural and honorable manner; the most sensitive conscience cannot take exception to it."

So saying, Madame de Reybert, nee de Corroy, stood erect as a pike-staff. She presented to the rapid investigation of the count a face seamed with the small-pox like a colander with holes, a flat, spare figure, two light and eager eyes, fair hair plastered down upon an anxious forehead, a small drawn-bonnet of faded green taffetas lined with pink, a white gown with violet spots, and leather shoes. The count recognized the wife of some poor, half-pay captain, a puritan, subscribing no doubt to the "Courrier Francais," earnest in virtue, but aware of the comfort of a good situation and eagerly coveting it.

"You say your husband has a pension of six hundred francs," he said, replying to his own thoughts, and not to the remark Madame de Reybert had just made.

"Yes, monsieur."

"You were born a Corroy?"

"Yes, monsieur,—a noble family of Metz, where my husband belongs."

"In what regiment did Monsieur de Reybert serve?"

"The 7th artillery."

"Good!" said the count, writing down the number.

He had thought at one time of giving the management of the estate to some retired army officer, about whom he could obtain exact information from the minister of war.

"Madame," he resumed, ringing for his valet, "return to Presles, this afternoon with my notary, who is going down there for dinner, and to whom I have recommended you. Here is his address. I am going myself secretly to Presles, and will send for Monsieur de Reybert to come and speak to me."

It will thus be seen that Monsieur de Serizy's journey by a public conveyance, and the injunction conveyed by the valet to conceal his name and rank had not unnecessarily alarmed Pierrotin. That worthy had just forebodings of a danger which was about to swoop down upon one of his best customers.

# CHAPTER III

## THE TRAVELLERS

As Pierrotin issued from the Cafe de l'Echiquier, after treating the valet, he saw in the gate-way of the Lion d'Argent the lady and the young man in whom his perspicacity at once detected customers, for the lady with outstretched neck and anxious face was evidently looking for him. She was dressed in a black-silk gown that was dyed, a brown bonnet, an old French cashmere shawl, raw-silk stockings, and low shoes; and in her hand she carried a straw bag and a blue umbrella. This woman, who had once been beautiful, seemed to be about forty years of age; but her blue eyes, deprived of the fire which happiness puts there, told plainly that she had long renounced the world. Her dress, as well as her whole air and demeanor, indicated a mother wholly devoted to her household and her son. If the strings of her bonnet were faded, the shape betrayed that it was several years old. The shawl was fastened by a broken needle converted into a pin by a bead of sealing-wax. She was waiting impatiently for Pierrotin, wishing to recommend to his special care her son, who was doubtless travelling for the first time, and with whom she had come to the coach-office as much from doubt of his ability as from maternal affection.

This mother was in every way completed by the son, so that the son would not be understood without the mother. If the mother condemned herself to mended gloves, the son wore an olive-green coat with sleeves too short for him, proving that he had grown, and might grow still more, like other adults of eighteen or nineteen years of age. The blue trousers, mended by his mother, presented to the eye a brighter patch of color when the coat-tails maliciously parted behind him.

"Don't rub your gloves that way, you'll spoil them," she was saying as Pierrotin appeared. "Is this the conductor? Ah! Pierrotin, is it you?" she exclaimed, leaving her son and taking the coachman apart a few steps.

"I hope you're well, Madame Clapart," he replied, with an air that expressed both respect and familiarity.

"Yes, Pierrotin, very well. Please take good care of my Oscar; he is travelling alone for the first time."

"Oh! so he is going alone to Monsieur Moreau!" cried Pierrotin, for the purpose of finding out whether he were really going there.

"Yes," said the mother.

"Then Madame Moreau is willing?" returned Pierrotin, with a sly look.

"Ah!" said the mother, "it will not be all roses for him, poor child! But his future absolutely requires that I should send him."

This answer struck Pierrotin, who hesitated to confide his fears for the steward to Madame Clapart, while she, on her part, was afraid of injuring her boy if she asked Pierrotin for a care which might have transformed him into a mentor. During this short deliberation, which was ostensibly covered by a few phrases as to the weather, the journey, and the stopping-places along the road, we will ourselves explain what were the ties that united Madame Clapart with Pierrotin, and authorized the two confidential remarks which they have just exchanged.

Often—that is to say, three or four times a month—Pierrotin, on his way to Paris, would find the steward on the road near La Cave. As soon as the vehicle came up, Moreau would sign to a gardener, who, with Pierrotin's help, would put upon the coach either one or two baskets containing the fruits and vegetables of the season, chickens, eggs, butter, and game. The steward always paid the carriage and Pierrotin's fee, adding the money necessary to pay the toll at the barriere, if the baskets contained anything dutiable. These baskets, hampers, or packages, were never directed to any one. On the first occasion, which served for all others, the steward had given Madame Clapart's address by word of mouth to the discreet Pierrotin, requesting him never to deliver to others the precious packages. Pierrotin, impressed with the idea of an intrigue between the steward and some pretty girl, had gone as directed to number 7 rue de la Cerisaie, in the Arsenal quarter, and had there found the Madame Clapart just portrayed, instead of the young and beautiful creature he expected to find.

The drivers of public conveyances and carriers are called by their business to enter many homes, and to be cognizant of many secrets; but social accident, that sub-providence, having willed that they be without education and devoid of the talent of observation, it follows that they are not dangerous. Nevertheless, at the end of a few months, Pierrotin was puzzled to explain the exact relations of Monsieur Moreau and Madame Clapart from what he saw of the household in the rue de la Cerisaie. Though lodgings were not dear at that time in the Arsenal quarter, Madame Clapart lived on a third floor at the end of a court-yard, in a house which was formerly that of a great family, in the days when the higher nobility of the kingdom lived on the ancient site of the Palais des Tournelles and the hotel Saint-Paul. Toward the end of the sixteenth century, the great seigneurs divided among themselves these vast spaces, once occupied by the gardens of the kings of France, as indicated by the present names of the streets,—Cerisaie, Beautreillis, des Lions, etc. Madame Clapart's apartment, which was panelled throughout with ancient carvings, consisted of three connecting rooms, a dining-room, salon, and bedroom. Above it was the kitchen, and a bedroom for Oscar. Opposite to the entrance, on what is called in Paris "le carre,"—that is, the square landing,—was the door of a back room, opening, on every floor, into a sort of tower built of rough stone, in which was also the well for the staircase. This was the room in which Moreau slept whenever he went to Paris.

Pierrotin had seen in the first room, where he deposited the hampers, six wooden chairs with straw seats, a table, and a sideboard; at the windows, discolored curtains. Later, when he entered the salon, he noticed some old Empire furniture, now shabby; but only as much as all proprietors exact to secure their rent. Pierrotin judged of the bedroom by the salon and dining-room. The wood-work, painted coarsely of a reddish white, which thickened and blurred the mouldings and figurines, far from being ornamental, was distressing to the eye. The floors, never waxed, were of that gray tone we see in boarding-schools. When Pierrotin came upon Monsieur and Madame Clapart at their meals he saw that their china, glass, and all other little articles betrayed the utmost poverty; and yet, though the chipped and mended dishes and tureens were those of the poorest families and provoked pity, the forks and spoons were of silver.

Monsieur Clapart, clothed in a shabby surtout, his feet in broken slippers, always wore green spectacles, and exhibited, whenever he removed his shabby cap of a bygone period, a pointed skull, from the top of which trailed a few dirty filaments which even a poet could scarcely call hair. This man, of wan complexion, seemed timorous, but withal tyrannical.

In this dreary apartment, which faced the north and had no other outlook than to a vine on the opposite wall and a well in the corner of the yard, Madame Clapart bore herself with the airs of a queen, and moved like a woman unaccustomed to go anywhere on foot. Often, while thanking Pierrotin, she gave him glances which would have touched to pity an intelligent observer; from time to time she would slip a twelve-sous piece into his hand, and then her voice was charming. Pierrotin had never seen Oscar, for the reason that the boy was always in school at the time his business took him to the house.

Here is the sad story which Pierrotin could never have discovered, even by asking for information, as he sometimes did, from the portress of the house; for that individual knew nothing beyond the fact that the Claparts paid a rent of two hundred and fifty francs a year, had no servant but a charwoman who came daily for a few hours in the morning, that Madame Clapart did some of her smaller washing herself, and paid the postage on her letters daily, being apparently unable to let the sum accumulate.

There does not exist, or rather, there seldom exists, a criminal who is wholly criminal. Neither do we ever meet with a dishonest nature which is completely dishonest. It is possible for a man to cheat his master to his own advantage, or rake in for himself alone all the hay in the manger, but, even while laying up capital by actions more or less illicit, there are few men who never do good ones. If only from self-love, curiosity, or by way of variety, or by chance, every man has his moment of beneficence; he may call it his error, he may never do it again, but he sacrifices to Goodness, as the most surly man sacrifices to the Graces once or twice in his life. If Moreau's faults can ever be excused, it might be on the score of his persistent kindness in succoring a woman of whose favors he had once been proud, and in whose house he was hidden when in peril of his life.

This woman, celebrated under the Directory for her liaison with one of the five kings of that reign, married, through that all-powerful protection, a purveyor who was making his millions out of the government, and whom Napoleon ruined in 1802. This man, named Husson, became insane through his sudden fall from opulence to poverty; he flung himself into the Seine, leaving the beautiful Madame Husson pregnant. Moreau, very intimately allied with Madame Husson, was at that time condemned to death; he was unable therefore to marry the widow, being forced to leave France. Madame Husson, then twenty-two years old, married in her deep distress a government clerk named Clapart, aged twenty-seven, who was said to be a rising man. At that period of our history, government clerks were apt to become persons of importance; for Napoleon was ever on the lookout for capacity. But Clapart, though endowed by nature with a certain coarse beauty, proved to have no intelligence. Thinking Madame Husson very rich, he feigned a great passion for her, and was simply saddled with the impossibility of satisfying either then or in the future the wants she had acquired in a life of opulence. He filled, very poorly, a place in the Treasury that gave him a salary of eighteen hundred francs; which was all the new household had to live on. When Moreau returned to France as the secretary of the Comte de Serizy he heard of Madame Husson's pitiable condition, and he was able, before his own marriage, to get her an appointment as head-waiting-woman to Madame Mere, the Emperor's mother. But in spite of that powerful protection Clapart was never promoted; his incapacity was too apparent.

Ruined in 1815 by the fall of the Empire, the brilliant Aspasia of the Directory had no other resources than Clapart's salary of twelve hundred francs from a clerkship obtained for him through the Comte de Serizy. Moreau, the only protector of a woman whom he had known in possession of millions, obtained a half-scholarship for her son, Oscar Husson, at the school of Henri IV.; and he sent her regularly, by Pierrotin, such supplies from the estate at Presles as he could decently offer to a household in distress.

Oscar was the whole life and all the future of his mother. The poor woman could now be reproached with no other fault than her exaggerated tenderness for her boy,—the bete-noire of his step-father. Oscar was, unfortunately, endowed by nature with a foolishness his mother did not perceive, in spite of the step-father's sarcasms. This foolishness—or, to speak more specifically, this overweening conceit—so troubled Monsieur Moreau that he begged Madame Clapart to send the boy down to him for a month that he might study his character, and find out what career he was fit for. Moreau was really thinking of some day proposing Oscar to the count as his successor.

But to give to the devil and to God what respectively belongs to them, perhaps it would be well to show the causes of Oscar Husson's silly self-conceit, premising that he was born in the household of Madame Mere. During his early childhood his eyes were dazzled by imperial splendors. His pliant imagination retained the impression of those gorgeous scenes, and nursed the images of a golden time of pleasure in hopes of recovering them. The natural boastfulness of school-boys (possessed of a desire to outshine their mates) resting on these memories of his childhood was developed in him beyond all measure. It may also have been that his mother at home dwelt too fondly on the days when she herself was a queen in Directorial Paris. At any rate, Oscar, who was now leaving school, had been made to bear many humiliations which the paying pupils put upon those who hold scholarships, unless the scholars are able to impose respect by superior physical ability.

This mixture of former splendor now departed, of beauty gone, of blind maternal love, of sufferings heroically borne, made the mother one of those pathetic figures which catch the eye of many an observer in Paris.

Incapable, naturally, of understanding the real attachment of Moreau to this woman, or that of the woman for the man she had saved in 1797, now her only friend, Pierrotin did not think it best to communicate the suspicion that had entered his head as to some danger which was threatening Moreau. The valet's speech, "We have enough to do in this world to look after ourselves," returned to his mind, and with it came that sentiment of obedience to what he called the "chefs de file,"—the front-rank men in war, and men of rank in peace. Besides, just now Pierrotin's head was as full of his own stings as there are five-franc pieces in a thousand francs. So that the "Very good, madame," "Certainly, madame," with which he replied to the poor mother, to whom a trip of twenty miles appeared a journey, showed plainly that he desired to get away from her useless and prolix instructions.

"You will be sure to place the packages so that they cannot get wet if the weather should happen to change."

"I've a hood," replied Pierrotin. "Besides, see, madame, with what care they are being placed."

"Oscar, don't stay more than two weeks, no matter how much they may ask you," continued Madame Clapart, returning to her son. "You can't please Madame Moreau, whatever you do; besides, you must be home by the end of September. We are to go to Belleville, you know, to your uncle Cardot."

"Yes, mamma."

"Above all," she said, in a low voice, "be sure never to speak about servants; keep thinking all the time that Madame Moreau was once a waiting-maid."

"Yes, mamma."

Oscar, like all youths whose vanity is excessively ticklish, seemed annoyed at being lectured on the threshold of the Lion d'Argent.

"Well, now good-bye, mamma. We shall start soon; there's the horse all harnessed."

The mother, forgetting that she was in the open street, embraced her Oscar, and said, smiling, as she took a little roll from her basket:—

"Tiens! you were forgetting your roll and the chocolate! My child, once more, I repeat, don't take anything at the inns; they'd make you pay for the slightest thing ten times what it is worth."

Oscar would fain have seen his mother farther off as she stuffed the bread and chocolate into his pocket. The scene had two witnesses,—two young men a few years older than Oscar, better dressed than he, without a mother hanging on to them, whose actions, dress, and ways all betokened that complete independence which is the one desire of a lad still tied to his mother's apron-strings.

"He said *mamma!*" cried one of the new-comers, laughing.

The words reached Oscar's ears and drove him to say, "Good-bye, mother!" in a tone of terrible impatience.

Let us admit that Madame Clapart spoke too loudly, and seemed to wish to show to those around them her tenderness for the boy.

"What is the matter with you, Oscar?" asked the poor hurt woman. "I don't know what to make of you," she added in a severe tone, fancying herself able to inspire him with respect,—a great mistake made by those who spoil their children. "Listen, my Oscar," she said, resuming at once her tender voice, "you have a propensity to talk, and to tell all you know, and all that you don't know; and you do it to show off, with the foolish vanity of a mere lad. Now, I repeat, endeavor to keep your tongue in check. You are not sufficiently advanced in life, my treasure, to be able to judge of the persons with whom you may be thrown; and there is nothing more dangerous than to talk in public conveyances. Besides, in a diligence well-bred persons always keep silence."

The two young men, who seemed to have walked to the farther end of the establishment, here returned, making their boot-heels tap upon the paved passage of the porte-cochere. They might have heard the whole of this maternal homily. So, in order to rid himself of his mother, Oscar had recourse to an heroic measure, which proved how vanity stimulates the intellect.

"Mamma," he said, "you are standing in a draught, and you may take cold. Besides, I am going to get into the coach."

The lad must have touched some tender spot, for his mother caught him to her bosom, kissed him as if he were starting upon a long journey, and went with him to the vehicle with tears in her eyes.

"Don't forget to give five francs to the servants when you come away," she said; "write me three times at least during the fifteen days; behave properly, and remember all that I have told you. You have linen enough; don't send any to the wash. And above all, remember Monsieur Moreau's kindness; mind him as you would a father, and follow his advice."

As he got into the coach, Oscar's blue woollen stockings became visible, through the action of his trousers which drew up suddenly, also the new patch in the said trousers was seen, through the parting of his coat-tails. The smiles of the two young men, on whom these signs of an honorable indigence were not lost, were so many fresh wounds to the lad's vanity.

"The first place was engaged for Oscar," said the mother to Pierrotin. "Take the back seat," she said to the boy, looking fondly at him with a loving smile.

Oh! how Oscar regretted that trouble and sorrow had destroyed his mother's beauty, and that poverty and self-sacrifice prevented her from being better dressed! One of the young men, the one who wore top-boots and spurs, nudged the other to make him take notice of Oscar's mother, and the other twirled his moustache with a gesture which signified,—

"Rather pretty figure!"

"How shall I ever get rid of mamma?" thought Oscar.

"What's the matter?" asked Madame Clapart.

Oscar pretended not to hear, the monster! Perhaps Madame Clapart was lacking in tact under the circumstances; but all absorbing sentiments have so much egotism!

"Georges, do you like children when travelling?" asked one young man of the other.

"Yes, my good Amaury, if they are weaned, and are named Oscar, and have chocolate."

These speeches were uttered in half-tones to allow Oscar to hear them or not hear them as he chose; his countenance was to be the weather-gauge by which the other young traveller could judge how much fun he might be able to get out of the lad during the journey. Oscar chose not to hear. He looked to see if his mother, who weighed upon him like a nightmare, was still there, for he felt that she loved him too well to leave him so quickly. Not only did he involuntarily compare the dress of his travelling companion with his own, but he felt that his mother's toilet counted for much in the smiles of the two young men.

"If they would only take themselves off!" he said to himself.

Instead of that, Amaury remarked to Georges, giving a tap with his cane to the heavy wheel of the coucou:

"And so, my friend, you are really going to trust your future to this fragile bark?"

"I must," replied Georges, in a tone of fatalism.

Oscar gave a sigh as he remarked the jaunty manner in which his companion's hat was stuck on one ear for the purpose of showing a magnificent head of blond hair beautifully brushed and curled; while he, by order of his step-father, had his black hair cut like a clothes-brush across the forehead, and clipped, like a soldier's, close to the head. The face of the vain lad was round and chubby and bright with the hues of health, while that of his fellow-traveller was long, and delicate, and pale. The forehead of the latter was broad, and his chest filled out a waistcoat of cashmere pattern. As Oscar admired the tight-fitting iron-gray trousers and the overcoat with its frogs and olives clasping the waist, it seemed to him that this romantic-looking stranger, gifted with such advantages, insulted him by his superiority, just as an ugly woman feels injured by the mere sight of a pretty one. The click of the stranger's boot-heels offended his taste and echoed in his heart. He felt as hampered by his own clothes (made no doubt at home out of those of his step-father) as that envied young man seemed at ease in his.

"That fellow must have heaps of francs in his trousers pocket," thought Oscar.

The young man turned round. What were Oscar's feelings on beholding a gold chain round his neck, at the end of which no doubt was a gold watch! From that moment the young man assumed, in Oscar's eyes, the proportions of a personage.

Living in the rue de la Cerisaie since 1815, taken to and from school by his step-father, Oscar had no other points of comparison since his adolescence than the poverty-stricken household of his mother. Brought up strictly, by Moreau's advice, he seldom went to the theatre, and then to nothing better than the Ambigu-Comique, where his eyes could see little elegance, if indeed the eyes of a child riveted on a melodrama were likely to examine the audience. His step-father still wore, after the fashion of the Empire, his watch in the fob of his trousers, from which there depended over his abdomen a heavy gold chain, ending in a bunch of heterogeneous ornaments, seals, and a watch-key with a round top and flat sides, on which was a landscape in mosaic. Oscar, who considered that old-fashioned finery as the "ne plus ultra" of adornment, was bewildered by the present revelation of superior and negligent elegance. The young man exhibited, offensively, a pair of spotless gloves, and seemed to wish to dazzle Oscar by twirling with much grace a gold-headed switch cane.

Oscar had reached that last quarter of adolescence when little things cause immense joys and immense miseries,—a period when youth prefers misfortune to a ridiculous suit of clothes, and caring nothing for the real interests of life, torments itself about frivolities, about neckcloths, and the passionate desire to appear a man. Then the young fellow swells himself out; his swagger is all the more portentous because it is exercised on nothings. Yet if he envies a fool who is elegantly dressed, he is also capable of enthusiasm over talent, and of genuine admiration for genius. Such defects as these, when they have no root in the heart, prove only the exuberance of sap,—the richness of the youthful imagination. That a lad of nineteen, an only child, kept severely at home by poverty, adored by a mother who put upon herself all privations for his sake, should be moved to envy by a young man of twenty-two in a frogged surtout-coat silk-lined, a waist-coat of fancy cashmere, and a cravat slipped through a ring of the worse taste, is nothing more than a peccadillo committed in all ranks of social life by inferiors who envy those that seem beyond them. Men of genius themselves succumb to this primitive passion. Did not Rousseau admire Ventura and Bacle?

But Oscar passed from peccadillo to evil feelings. He felt humiliated; he was angry with the youth he envied, and there rose in his heart a secret desire to show openly that he himself was as good as the object of his envy.

The two young fellows continued to walk up and own from the gate to the stables, and from the stables to the gate. Each time they turned they looked at Oscar curled up in his corner of the coucou. Oscar, persuaded that their jokes and laughter concerned himself, affected the utmost indifference. He began to hum the chorus of a song lately brought into vogue by the liberals, which ended with the words, "'Tis Voltaire's fault, 'tis Rousseau's fault."

"Tiens! perhaps he is one of the chorus at the Opera," said Amaury.

This exasperated Oscar, who bounded up, pulled out the wooden "back," and called to Pierrotin:—

"When do we start?"

"Presently," said that functionary, who was standing, whip in hand, and gazing toward the rue d'Enghien.

At this moment the scene was enlivened by the arrival of a young man accompanied by a true "gamin," who was followed by a porter dragging a hand-cart. The young man came up to Pierrotin and spoke to him confidentially, on which the latter nodded his head, and called to his own porter. The man ran out and helped to unload the little hand-cart, which contained, besides two trunks, buckets, brushes, boxes of singular shape, and an infinity of packages and utensils which the youngest of the new-comers, who had climbed into the imperial, stowed away with such celerity that Oscar, who happened to be smiling at his mother, now standing on the other side of the street, saw none of the paraphernalia which might have revealed to him the profession of his new travelling companion.

The gamin, who must have been sixteen years of age, wore a gray blouse buckled round his waist by a polished leather belt. His cap, jauntily perched on the side of his head, seemed the sign of a merry nature, and so did the picturesque disorder of the curly brown hair which fell upon his shoulders. A black-silk cravat drew a line round his very white neck, and added to the vivacity of his bright gray eyes. The animation of his brown and rosy face, the moulding of his rather large lips, the ears detached from his head, his slightly turned-up nose,—in fact, all the details of his face proclaimed the lively spirit of a Figaro, and the careless gayety of youth, while the vivacity of his gesture and his mocking eye revealed an intellect already developed by the practice of a profession adopted very early in life. As he had already some claims to personal value, this child, made man by Art or by vocation, seemed indifferent to the question of costume; for he looked at his boots, which had not been polished, with a quizzical air, and searched for the spots on his brown Holland trousers less to remove them than to see their effect.

"I'm in style," he said, giving himself a shake and addressing his companion.

The glance of the latter, showed authority over his adept, in whom a practised eye would at once have recognized the joyous pupil of a painter, called in the argot of the studios a "rapin."

"Behave yourself, Mistigris," said his master, giving him the nickname which the studio had no doubt bestowed upon him.

The master was a slight and pale young man, with extremely thick black hair, worn in a disorder that was actually fantastic. But this abundant mass of hair seemed necessary to an enormous head, whose vast forehead proclaimed a precocious intellect. A strained and harassed face, too original to be ugly, was hollowed as if this noticeable young man suffered from some chronic malady, or from privations caused by poverty (the most terrible of all chronic maladies), or from griefs too recent to be forgotten. His clothing, analogous, with due allowance, to that of Mistigris, consisted of a shabby surtout coat, American-green in color, much worn, but clean and well-brushed; a black waistcoat buttoned to the throat, which almost concealed a scarlet neckerchief; and trousers, also black and even more worn than the coat, flapping his thin legs. In addition, a pair of very muddy boots indicated that he had come on foot and from some distance to the coach office. With a rapid look this artist seized the whole scene of the Lion d'Argent, the stables, the courtyard, the various lights and shades, and the details; then he looked at Mistigris, whose satirical glance had followed his own.

"Charming!" said Mistigris.

"Yes, very," replied the other.

"We seem to have got here too early," pursued Mistigris. "Couldn't we get a mouthful somewhere? My stomach, like Nature, abhors a vacuum."

"Have we time to get a cup of coffee?" said the artist, in a gentle voice, to Pierrotin.

"Yes, but don't be long," answered the latter.

"Good; that means we have a quarter of an hour," remarked Mistigris, with the innate genius for observation of the Paris rapin.

The pair disappeared. Nine o'clock was striking in the hotel kitchen. Georges thought it just and reasonable to remonstrate with Pierrotin.

"Hey! my friend; when a man is blessed with such wheels as these (striking the clumsy tires with his cane) he ought at least to have the merit of punctuality. The deuce! one doesn't get into that thing for pleasure; I have business that is devilishly pressing or I wouldn't trust my bones to it. And that horse, which you call Rougeot, he doesn't look likely to make up for lost time."

"We are going to harness Bichette while those gentlemen take their coffee," replied Pierrotin. "Go and ask, you," he said to his porter, "if Pere Leger is coming with us—"

"Where is your Pere Leger?" asked Georges.

"Over the way, at number 50. He couldn't get a place in the Beaumont diligence," said Pierrotin, still speaking to his porter and apparently making no answer to his customer; then he disappeared himself in search of Bichette.

Georges, after shaking hands with his friend, got into the coach, handling with an air of great importance a portfolio which he placed beneath the cushion of the seat. He took the opposite corner to that of Oscar, on the same seat.

"This Pere Leger troubles me," he said.

"They can't take away our places," replied Oscar. "I have number one."

"And I number two," said Georges.

Just as Pierrotin reappeared, having harnessed Bichette, the porter returned with a stout man in tow, whose weight could not have been less than two hundred and fifty pounds at the very least. Pere Leger belonged to the species of farmer which has a square back, a protuberant stomach, a powdered pigtail, and wears a little coat of blue linen. His white gaiters, coming above the knee, were fastened round the ends of his velveteen breeches and secured by silver buckles. His hob-nailed shoes weighed two pounds each. In his hand, he held a small reddish stick, much polished, with a large knob, which was fastened round his wrist by a thong of leather.

"And you are called Pere Leger?" asked Georges, very seriously, as the farmer attempted to put a foot on the step.

"At your service," replied the farmer, looking in and showing a face like that of Louis XVIII., with fat, rubicund cheeks, from between which issued a nose that in any other face would have seemed enormous. His smiling eyes were sunken in rolls of fat. "Come, a helping hand, my lad!" he said to Pierrotin.

The farmer was hoisted in by the united efforts of Pierrotin and the porter, to cries of "Houp la! hi! ha! hoist!" uttered by Georges.

"Oh! I'm not going far; only to La Cave," said the farmer, good-humoredly.

In France everybody takes a joke.

"Take the back seat," said Pierrotin, "there'll be six of you."

"Where's your other horse?" demanded Georges. "Is it as mythical as the third post-horse."

"There she is," said Pierrotin, pointing to the little mare, who was coming along alone.

"He calls that insect a horse!" exclaimed Georges.

"Oh! she's good, that little mare," said the farmer, who by this time was seated. "Your servant, gentlemen. Well, Pierrotin, how soon do you start?"

"I have two travellers in there after a cup of coffee," replied Pierrotin.

The hollow-cheeked young man and his page reappeared.

"Come, let's start!" was the general cry.

"We are going to start," replied Pierrotin. "Now, then, make ready," he said to the porter, who began thereupon to take away the stones which stopped the wheels.

Pierrotin took Rougeot by the bridle and gave that guttural cry, "Ket, ket!" to tell the two animals to collect their energy; on which, though evidently stiff, they pulled the coach to the door of the Lion d'Argent. After which manoeuvre, which was purely preparatory, Pierrotin gazed up the rue d'Enghien and then disappeared, leaving the coach in charge of the porter.

"Ah ca! is he subject to such attacks,—that master of yours?" said Mistigris, addressing the porter.

"He has gone to fetch his feed from the stable," replied the porter, well versed in all the usual tricks to keep passengers quiet.

"Well, after all," said Mistigris, "'art is long, but life is short'—to Bichette."

At this particular epoch, a fancy for mutilating or transposing proverbs reigned in the studios. It was thought a triumph to find changes of letters, and sometimes of words, which still kept the semblance of the proverb while giving it a fantastic or ridiculous meaning.*

"Patience, Mistigris!" said his master; "'come wheel, come whoa.'"

Pierrotin here returned, bringing with him the Comte de Serizy, who had come through the rue de l'Echiquier, and with whom he had doubtless had a short conversation.

"Pere Leger," said Pierrotin, looking into the coach, "will you give your place to Monsieur le comte? That will balance the carriage better."

"We sha'n't be off for an hour if you go on this way," cried Georges. "We shall have to take down this infernal bar, which cost such trouble to put up. Why should everybody be made to move for the man who comes last? We all have a right to the places we took. What place has monsieur

---

* It is plainly impossible to translate many of these proverbs and put any fun or meaning into them.—Tr.

engaged? Come, find that out! Haven't you a way-book, a register, or something? What place has Monsieur Lecomte engaged?—count of what, I'd like to know."

"Monsieur le comte," said Pierrotin, visibly troubled, "I am afraid you will be uncomfortable."

"Why didn't you keep better count of us?" said Mistigris. "'Short counts make good ends.'"

"Mistigris, behave yourself," said his master.

Monsieur de Serizy was evidently taken by all the persons in the coach for a bourgeois of the name of Lecomte.

"Don't disturb any one," he said to Pierrotin. "I will sit with you in front."

"Come, Mistigris," said the master to his rapin, "remember the respect you owe to age; you don't know how shockingly old you may be yourself some day. 'Travel deforms youth.' Give your place to monsieur."

Mistigris opened the leathern curtain and jumped out with the agility of a frog leaping into the water.

"You mustn't be a rabbit, august old man," he said to the count.

"Mistigris, 'ars est celare bonum,'" said his master.

"I thank you very much, monsieur," said the count to Mistigris's master, next to whom he now sat.

The minister of State cast a sagacious glance round the interior of the coach, which greatly affronted both Oscar and Georges.

"When persons want to be master of a coach, they should engage all the places," remarked Georges.

Certain now of his incognito, the Comte de Serizy made no reply to this observation, but assumed the air of a good-natured bourgeois.

"Suppose you were late, wouldn't you be glad that the coach waited for you?" said the farmer to the two young men.

Pierrotin still looked up and down the street, whip in hand, apparently reluctant to mount to the hard seat where Mistigris was fidgeting.

"If you expect some one else, I am not the last," said the count.

"I agree to that reasoning," said Mistigris.

Georges and Oscar began to laugh impertinently.

"The old fellow doesn't know much," whispered Georges to Oscar, who was delighted at this apparent union between himself and the object of his envy.

"Parbleu!" cried Pierrotin, "I shouldn't be sorry for two more passengers."

"I haven't paid; I'll get out," said Georges, alarmed.

"What are you waiting for, Pierrotin?" asked Pere Leger.

Whereupon Pierrotin shouted a certain "Hi!" in which Bichette and Rougeot recognized a definitive resolution, and they both sprang toward the rise of the faubourg at a pace which was soon to slacken.

The count had a red face, of a burning red all over, on which were certain inflamed portions which his snow-white hair brought out into full relief. To any but heedless youths, this complexion would have revealed a constant inflammation of the blood, produced by incessant labor. These blotches and pimples so injured the naturally noble air of the count that careful examination was needed to find in his green-gray eyes the shrewdness of the magistrate, the wisdom of a statesman, and the knowledge of a legislator. His face was flat, and the nose seemed to have been depressed into it. The hat hid the grace and beauty of his forehead. In short, there was enough to amuse those thoughtless youths in the odd contrasts of the silvery hair, the burning face, and the thick, tufted eye-brows which were still jet-black.

The count wore a long blue overcoat, buttoned in military fashion to the throat, a white cravat around his neck, cotton wool in his ears, and a shirt-collar high enough to make a large square patch of white on each cheek. His black trousers covered his boots, the toes of which were barely seen. He wore no decoration in his button-hole, and doeskin gloves concealed his hands. Nothing about him betrayed to the eyes of youth a peer of France, and one of the most useful statesmen in the kingdom.

Pere Leger had never seen the count, who, on his side, knew the former only by name. When the count, as he got into the carriage, cast the glance about him which affronted Georges and Oscar, he was, in reality, looking for the head-clerk of his notary (in case he had been forced, like himself, to take Pierrotin's vehicle), intending to caution him instantly about his own incognito. But feeling reassured by the appearance of Oscar, and that of Pere Leger, and, above all, by the quasi-military air, the waxed moustaches, and the general look of an adventurer that distinguished Georges, he concluded that his note had reached his notary, Alexandre Crottat, in time to prevent the departure of the clerk.

"Pere Leger," said Pierrotin, when they reached the steep hill of the faubourg Saint-Denis by the rue de la Fidelite, "suppose we get out, hey?"

"I'll get out, too," said the count, hearing Leger's name.

"Goodness! if this is how we are going, we shall do fourteen miles in fifteen days!" cried Georges.

"It isn't my fault," said Pierrotin, "if a passenger wishes to get out."

"Ten louis for you if you keep the secret of my being here as I told you before," said the count in a low voice, taking Pierrotin by the arm.

"Oh, my thousand francs!" thought Pierrotin as he winked an eye at Monsieur de Serizy, which meant, "Rely on me."

Oscar and Georges stayed in the coach.

"Look here, Pierrotin, since Pierrotin you are," cried Georges, when the passengers were once more stowed away in the vehicle, "if you don't mean to go faster than this, say so! I'll pay my fare and take a post-horse at Saint-Denis, for I have important business on hand which can't be delayed."

"Oh! he'll go well enough," said Pere Leger. "Besides, the distance isn't great."

"I am never more than half an hour late," asserted Pierrotin.

"Well, you are not wheeling the Pope in this old barrow of yours," said Georges, "so, get on."

"Perhaps he's afraid of shaking monsieur," said Mistigris looking round at the count. "But you shouldn't have preferences, Pierrotin, it isn't right."

"Coucous and the Charter make all Frenchmen equals," said Georges.

"Oh! be easy," said Pere Leger; "we are sure to get to La Chapelle by mid-day,"—La Chapelle being the village next beyond the Barriere of Saint-Denis.

# CHAPTER IV

# THE GRANDSON OF THE FAMOUS CZERNI-GEORGES

Those who travel in public conveyances know that the persons thus united by chance do not immediately have anything to say to one another; unless under special circumstances, conversation rarely begins until they have gone some distance. This period of silence is employed as much in mutual examination as in settling into their places. Minds need to get their equilibrium as much as bodies. When each person thinks he has discovered the age, profession, and character of his companions, the most talkative member of the company begins, and the conversation gets under way with all the more vivacity because those present feel a need of enlivening the journey and forgetting its tedium.

That is how things happen in French stage-coaches. In other countries customs are very different. Englishmen pique themselves on never opening their lips; Germans are melancholy in a vehicle; Italians too wary to talk; Spaniards have no public conveyances; and Russians no roads. There is no amusement except in the lumbering diligences of France, that gabbling and indiscreet country, where every one is in a hurry to laugh and show his wit, and where jest and epigram enliven all things, even the poverty of the lower classes and the weightier cares of the solid bourgeois. In a coach there is no police to check tongues, and legislative assemblies have set the fashion of public discussion. When a young man of twenty-two, like the one named Georges, is clever and lively, he is much tempted, especially under circumstances like the present, to abuse those qualities.

In the first place, Georges had soon decided that he was the superior human being of the party there assembled. He saw in the count a manufacturer of the second-class, whom he took, for some unknown reason, to be a chandler; in the shabby young man accompanied by Mistigris, a fellow of no account; in Oscar a ninny, and in Pere Leger, the fat farmer, an excellent subject to hoax. Having thus looked over the ground, he resolved to amuse himself at the expense of such companions.

"Let me see," he thought to himself, as the coucou went down the hill from La Chapelle to the plain of Saint-Denis, "shall I pass myself off for Etienne or Beranger? No, these idiots don't know who they are. Carbonaro? the deuce! I might get myself arrested. Suppose I say I'm the son of Marshal Ney? Pooh! what could I tell them?—about the execution of my father? It wouldn't be funny. Better be a disguised Russian prince and make them swallow a lot of stuff about the Emperor Alexander. Or I might be Cousin, and talk philosophy; oh, couldn't I perplex 'em! But no, that shabby fellow with the tousled head looks to me as if he had jogged his way through the Sorbonne. What a pity! I can mimic an Englishman so perfectly I might have pretended to be Lord Byron, travelling incognito. Sapristi! I'll command the troops of Ali, pacha of Janina!"

During this mental monologue, the coucou rolled through clouds of dust rising on either side of it from that much travelled road.

"What dust!" cried Mistigris.

"Henry IV. is dead!" retorted his master. "If you'd say it was scented with vanilla that would be emitting a new opinion."

"You think you're witty," replied Mistigris. "Well, it *is* like vanilla at times."

"In the Levant—" said Georges, with the air of beginning a story.

"'Ex Oriente flux,'" remarked Mistigris's master, interrupting the speaker.

60

"I said in the Levant, from which I have just returned," continued Georges, "the dust smells very good; but here it smells of nothing, except in some old dust-barrel like this."

"Has monsieur lately returned from the Levant?" said Mistigris, maliciously. "He isn't much tanned by the sun."

"Oh! I've just left my bed after an illness of three months, from the germ, so the doctors said, of suppressed plague."

"Have you had the plague?" cried the count, with a gesture of alarm. "Pierrotin, stop!"

"Go on, Pierrotin," said Mistigris. "Didn't you hear him say it was inward, his plague?" added the rapin, talking back to Monsieur de Serizy. "It isn't catching; it only comes out in conversation."

"Mistigris! if you interfere again I'll have you put off into the road," said his master. "And so," he added, turning to Georges, "monsieur has been to the East?"

"Yes, monsieur; first to Egypt, then to Greece, where I served under Ali, pacha of Janina, with whom I had a terrible quarrel. There's no enduring those climates long; besides, the emotions of all kinds in Oriental life have disorganized my liver."

"What, have you served as a soldier?" asked the fat farmer. "How old are you?"

"Twenty-nine," replied Georges, whereupon all the passengers looked at him. "At eighteen I enlisted as a private for the famous campaign of 1813; but I was present at only one battle, that of Hanau, where I was promoted sergeant-major. In France, at Montereau, I won the rank of sub-lieutenant, and was decorated by,—there are no informers here, I'm sure,—by the Emperor."

"What! are you decorated?" cried Oscar. "Why don't you wear your cross?"

"The cross of 'ceux-ci'? No, thank you! Besides, what man of any breeding would wear his decorations in travelling? There's monsieur," he said, motioning to the Comte de Serizy. "I'll bet whatever you like—"

"Betting whatever you like means, in France, betting nothing at all," said Mistigris's master.

"I'll bet whatever you like," repeated Georges, incisively, "that monsieur here is covered with stars."

"Well," said the count, laughing, "I have the grand cross of the Legion of honor, that of Saint Andrew of Russia, that of the Prussian Eagle, that of the Annunciation of Sardinia, and the Golden Fleece."

"Beg pardon," said Mistigris, "are they all in the coucou?"

"Hey! that brick-colored old fellow goes it strong!" whispered Georges to Oscar. "What was I saying?—oh! I know. I don't deny that I adore the Emperor—"

"I served under him," said the count.

"What a man he was, wasn't he?" cried Georges.

"A man to whom I owe many obligations," replied the count, with a silly expression that was admirably assumed.

"For all those crosses?" inquired Mistigris.

"And what quantities of snuff he took!" continued Monsieur de Serizy.

"He carried it loose in his pockets," said Georges.

"So I've been told," remarked Pere Leger with an incredulous look.

"Worse than that; he chewed and smoked," continued Georges. "I saw him smoking, in a queer way, too, at Waterloo, when Marshal Soult took him round the waist and flung him into his carriage, just as he had seized a musket and was going to charge the English—"

"You were at Waterloo!" cried Oscar, his eyes stretching wide open.

"Yes, young man, I did the campaign of 1815. I was a captain at Mont-Saint-Jean, and I retired to the Loire, after we were all disbanded. Faith! I was disgusted with France; I couldn't stand it. In fact, I should certainly have got myself arrested; so off I went, with two or three dashing fellows,—Selves, Besson, and others, who are now in Egypt,—and we entered the service of pacha Mohammed; a queer sort of fellow he was, too! Once a tobacco merchant in the bazaars, he is now on the high-road to be a sovereign prince. You've all seen him in that picture by Horace Vernet,—'The Massacre of the Mameluks.' What a handsome fellow he was! But I wouldn't give up the religion of my fathers and embrace Islamism; all the more because the abjuration required a surgical operation which I hadn't any fancy for. Besides, nobody respects a renegade. Now if they had offered me a hundred thousand francs a year, perhaps—and yet, no! The pacha did give me a thousand talari as a present."

"How much is that?" asked Oscar, who was listening to Georges with all his ears.

"Oh! not much. A talaro is, as you might say, a five-franc piece. But faith! I got no compensation for the vices I contracted in that God-forsaken country, if country it is. I can't live now without smoking a narghile twice a-day, and that's very costly."

"How did you find Egypt?" asked the count.

"Egypt? Oh! Egypt is all sand," replied Georges, by no means taken aback. "There's nothing green but the valley of the Nile. Draw a green line down a sheet of yellow paper, and you have Egypt. But those Egyptians—fellahs they are called—have an immense advantage over us. There are no gendarmes in that country. You may go from end to end of Egypt, and you won't see one."

"But I suppose there are a good many Egyptians," said Mistigris.

"Not as many as you think for," replied Georges. "There are many more Abyssinians, and Giaours, and Vechabites, Bedouins, and Cophs. But all that kind of animal is very uninteresting, and I was glad enough to embark on a Genoese polacca which was loading for the Ionian Islands with gunpowder and munitions for Ali de Tebelen. You know, don't you, that the British sell powder and munitions of war to all the world,—Turks, Greeks, and the devil, too, if the devil has money? From Zante we were to skirt the coasts of Greece and tack about, on and off. Now it happens that my name of Georges is famous in that country. I am, such as you see me, the grandson of the famous Czerni-Georges who made war upon the Porte, and, instead of crushing it, as he meant to do, got crushed himself. His son took refuge in the house of the French consul at Smyrna, and he afterwards died in Paris, leaving my mother pregnant with me, his seventh child. Our property was all stolen by friends of my grandfather; in fact, we were ruined. My mother, who lived on her diamonds, which she sold one by one, married, in 1799, my step-father, Monsieur Yung, a purveyor. But my mother is dead, and I have quarrelled with my step-father, who, between ourselves, is a blackguard; he is still alive, but I never see him. That's why, in despair, left all to myself, I went off to the wars as a private in 1813. Well, to go back to the time I returned to Greece; you wouldn't believe with what joy old Ali Tebelen received the grandson of Czerni-Georges. Here, of course, I call myself simply Georges. The pacha gave me a harem—"

"You have had a harem?" said Oscar.

"Were you a pacha with *many* tails?" asked Mistigris.

"How is it that you don't know," replied Georges, "that only the Sultan makes pachas, and that my friend Tebelen (for we were as friendly as Bourbons) was in rebellion against the Padishah! You know, or you don't know, that the true title of the Grand Seignior is Padishah, and not Sultan or Grand Turk. You needn't think that a harem is much of a thing; you might as well have a herd of goats. The women are horribly stupid down there; I much prefer the grisettes of the Chaumieres at Mont-Parnasse."

"They are nearer, at any rate," said the count.

"The women of the harem couldn't speak a word of French, and that language is indispensable for talking. Ali gave me five legitimate wives and ten slaves; that's equivalent to having none at all at Janina. In the East, you must know, it is thought very bad style to have wives and women. They have them, just as we have Voltaire and Rousseau; but who ever opens his Voltaire or his Rousseau? Nobody. But, for all that, the highest style is to be jealous. They sew a woman up in a sack and fling her into the water on the slightest suspicion,—that's according to their Code."

"Did you fling any in?" asked the farmer.

"I, a Frenchman! for shame! I loved them."

Whereupon Georges twirled and twisted his moustache with a dreamy air.

They were now entering Saint-Denis, and Pierrotin presently drew up before the door of a tavern where were sold the famous cheese-cakes of that place. All the travellers got out. Puzzled by the apparent truth mingled with Georges' inventions, the count returned to the coucou when the others had entered the house, and looked beneath the cushion for the portfolio which Pierrotin told him that enigmatical youth had placed there. On it he read the words in gilt letters: "Maitre Crottat, notary." The count at once opened it, and fearing, with some reason, that Pere Leger might be seized with the same curiosity, he took out the deed of sale for the farm at Moulineaux, put it into his coat pocket, and entered the inn to keep an eye on the travellers.

"This Georges is neither more nor less than Crottat's second clerk," thought he. "I shall pay my compliments to his master, whose business it was to send me his head-clerk."

From the respectful glances of Pere Leger and Oscar, Georges perceived that he had made for himself two fervent admirers. Accordingly, he now posed as a great personage; paid for their cheese-cakes, and ordered for each a glass of Alicante. He offered the same to Mistigris and his master, who refused with smiles; but the friend of Ali Tebelen profited by the occasion to ask the pair their names.

"Oh! monsieur," said Mistigris' master, "I am not blessed, like you, with an illustrious name; and I have not returned from Asia—"

At this moment the count, hastening into the huge inn-kitchen lest his absence should excite inquiry, entered the place in time to hear the conclusion of the young man's speech.

"—I am only a poor painter lately returned from Rome, where I went at the cost of the government, after winning the 'grand prix' five years ago. My name is Schinner."

"Hey! bourgeois, may I offer you a glass of Alicante and some cheese-cakes?" said Georges to the count.

"Thank you," replied the latter. "I never leave home without taking my cup of coffee and cream."

"Don't you eat anything between meals? How bourgeois, Marais, Place Royale, that is!" cried Georges. "When he 'blagued' just now about his crosses, I thought there was something in him," whispered the Eastern hero to the painter. "However, we'll set him going on his decorations, the old tallow-chandler! Come, my lad," he added, calling to Oscar, "drink me down the glass poured out for the chandler; that will start your moustache."

Oscar, anxious to play the man, swallowed the second glass of wine, and ate three more cheese-cakes.

"Good wine, that!" said Pere Leger, smacking his lips.

"It is all the better," said Georges, "because it comes from Bercy. I've been to Alicante myself, and I know that this wine no more resembles what is made there than my arm is like a windmill. Our made-up wines are a great deal better than the natural ones in their own country. Come, Pierrotin, take a glass! It is a great pity your horses can't take one, too; we might go faster."

"Forward, march!" cried Pierrotin, amid a mighty cracking of whips, after the travellers were again boxed up.

It was now eleven o'clock. The weather, which had been cloudy, cleared; the breeze swept off the mists, and the blue of the sky appeared in spots; so that when the coucou trundled along the narrow strip of road from Saint-Denis to Pierrefitte, the sun had fairly drunk up the last floating vapors of the diaphanous veil which swathed the scenery of that famous region.

"Well, now, tell us why you left your friend the pacha," said Pere Leger, addressing Georges.

"He was a very singular scamp," replied Georges, with an air that hid a multitude of mysteries. "He put me in command of his cavalry,—so far, so good—"

"Ah! that's why he wears spurs," thought poor Oscar.

"At that time Ali Tebelen wanted to rid himself of Chosrew pacha, another queer chap! You call him, here, Chaureff; but the name is pronounced, in Turkish, Cosserew. You must have read in the newspapers how old Ali drubbed Chosrew, and soundly, too, faith! Well, if it hadn't been for me, Ali Tebelen himself would have bit the dust two days earlier. I was at the right wing, and I saw Chosrew, an old sly-boots, thinking to force our centre,—ranks closed, stiff, swift, fine movement a la Murat. Good! I take my time; then I charge, double-quick, and cut his line in two,—you understand? Ha! ha! after the affair was over, Ali kissed me—"

"Do they do that in the East?" asked the count, in a joking way.

"Yes, monsieur," said the painter, "that's done all the world over."

"After that," continued Georges, "Ali gave me yataghans, and carbines, and scimetars, and what-not. But when we got back to his capital he made me propositions, wanted me to drown a wife, and make a slave of myself,—Orientals are so queer! But I thought I'd had enough of it; for, after all, you know, Ali was a rebel against the Porte. So I concluded I had better get off while I could. But I'll do Monsieur Tebelen the justice to say that he loaded me with presents,—diamonds, ten thousand talari, one thousand gold coins, a beautiful Greek girl for groom, a little Circassian for a mistress, and an Arab horse! Yes, Ali Tebelen, pacha of Janina, is too little known; he needs an historian. It is only in the East one meets with such iron souls, who can nurse a vengeance twenty years and accomplish it some fine morning. He had the most magnificent white beard that was ever seen, and a hard, stern face—"

"But what did you do with your treasures?" asked farmer Leger.

"Ha! that's it! you may well ask that! Those fellows down there haven't any Grand Livre nor any Bank of France. So I was forced to carry off my windfalls in a felucca, which was captured by the Turkish High-Admiral himself. Such as you see me here to-day, I came very near being impaled at Smyrna. Indeed, if it hadn't been for Monsieur de Riviere, our ambassador, who was there, they'd have taken me for an accomplice of Ali pacha. I saved my head, but, to tell the honest truth, all the rest, the ten thousand talari, the thousand gold pieces, and the fine weapons, were all, yes all, drunk up by the thirsty treasury of the Turkish admiral. My position was the more perilous because that very admiral happened to be Chosrew pacha. After I routed him, the fellow had managed to obtain a position which is equal to that of our Admiral of the Fleet—"

"But I thought he was in the cavalry?" said Pere Leger, who had followed the narrative with the deepest attention.

"Dear me! how little the East is understood in the French provinces!" cried Georges. "Monsieur, I'll explain the Turks to you. You are a farmer; the Padishah (that's the Sultan) makes you a marshal; if you don't fulfil your functions to his satisfaction, so much the worse for you, he cuts your head off; that's his way of dismissing his functionaries. A gardener is made a prefect; and the prime minister comes down to be a foot-boy. The Ottomans have no system of promotion and no hierarchy. From a cavalry officer Chosrew simply became a naval officer. Sultan Mahmoud ordered him to capture Ali by sea; and he did get hold of him, assisted by those beggarly English—who put their paw on most of the treasure. This Chosrew, who had not forgotten the riding-lesson I gave him, recognized me. You understand, my goose was cooked, oh, brown! when it suddenly came into my head to claim protection as a Frenchman and a troubadour from Monsieur de Riviere. The ambassador, enchanted to find something to show him off, demanded that I should be set at liberty. The Turks have one good trait in their nature; they are as willing to let you go as they are to cut your head off; they are indifferent to everything. The French consul, charming fellow, friend of Chosrew, made him give back two thousand of the talari, and, consequently, his name is, as I may say, graven on my heart—"

"What was his name?" asked Monsieur de Serizy; and a look of some surprise passed over his face as Georges named, correctly, one of our most distinguished consul-generals who happened at that time to be stationed at Smyrna.

"I assisted," added Georges, "at the execution of the Governor of Smyrna, whom the Sultan had ordered Chosrew to put to death. It was one of the most curious things I ever saw, though I've seen many,—I'll tell you about it when we stop for breakfast. From Smyrna I crossed to Spain, hearing there was a revolution there. I went straight to Mina, who appointed me as his aide-de-camp with the rank of colonel. I fought for the constitutional cause, which will certainly be defeated when we enter Spain—as we undoubtedly shall, some of these days—"

"You, a French soldier!" said the count, sternly. "You show extraordinary confidence in the discretion of those who are listening to you."

"But there are no spies here," said Georges.

"Are you aware, Colonel Georges," continued the count, "that the Court of Peers is at this very time inquiring into a conspiracy which has made the government extremely severe in its treatment of French soldiers who bear arms against France, and who deal in foreign intrigues for the purpose of overthrowing our legitimate sovereigns."

On hearing this stern admonition the painter turned red to his ears and looked at Mistigris, who seemed dumfounded.

"Well," said Pere Leger, "what next?"

"If," continued the count, "I were a magistrate, it would be my duty to order the gendarmes at Pierrefitte to arrest the aide-de-camp of Mina, and to summon all present in this vehicle to testify to his words."

This speech stopped Georges' narrative all the more surely, because at this moment the coucou reached the guard-house of a brigade of gendarmerie,—the white flag floating, as the orthodox saying is, upon the breeze.

"You have too many decorations to do such a dastardly thing," said Oscar.

"Never mind; we'll catch up with him soon," whispered Georges in the lad's ear.

"Colonel," cried Leger, who was a good deal disturbed by the count's outburst, and wanted to change the conversation, "in all these countries where you have been, what sort of farming do they do? How do they vary the crops?"

"Well, in the first place, my good fellow, you must understand, they are too busy cropping off each others' heads to think much of cropping the ground."

The count couldn't help smiling; and that smile reassured the narrator.

"They have a way of cultivating which you will think very queer. They don't cultivate at all; that's their style of farming. The Turks and the Greeks, they eat onions or rise. They get opium from poppies, and it gives them a fine revenue. Then they have tobacco, which grows of itself, famous latakiah! and dates! and all kinds of sweet things that don't need cultivation. It is a country full of resources and commerce. They make fine rugs at Smyrna, and not dear."

"But," persisted Leger, "if the rugs are made of wool they must come from sheep; and to have sheep you must have fields, farms, culture—"

"Well, there may be something of that sort," replied Georges. "But their chief crop, rice, grows in the water. As for me, I have only been along the coasts and seen the parts that are devastated by war. Besides, I have the deepest aversion to statistics."

"How about the taxes?" asked the farmer.

"Oh! the taxes are heavy; they take all a man has, and leave him the rest. The pacha of Egypt was so struck with the advantages of that system, that, when I came away he was on the point of organizing his own administration on that footing—"

"But," said Leger, who no longer understood a single word, "how?"

"How?" said Georges. "Why, agents go round and take all the harvests, and leave the fellahs just enough to live on. That's a system that does away with stamped papers and bureaucracy, the curse of France, hein?"

"By virtue of what right?" said Leger.

"Right? why it is a land of despotism. They haven't any rights. Don't you know the fine definition Montesquieu gives of despotism. 'Like the savage, it cuts down the tree to gather the fruits.' They don't tax, they take everything."

"And that's what our rulers are trying to bring us to. 'Tax vobiscum,'—no, thank you!" said Mistigris.

"But that is what we *are* coming to," said the count. "Therefore, those who own land will do well to sell it. Monsieur Schinner must have seen how things are tending in Italy, where the taxes are enormous."

"Corpo di Bacco! the Pope is laying it on heavily," replied Schinner. "But the people are used to it. Besides, Italians are so good-natured that if you let 'em murder a few travellers along the highways they're contented."

"I see, Monsieur Schinner," said the count, "that you are not wearing the decoration you obtained in 1819; it seems the fashion nowadays not to wear orders."

Mistigris and the pretended Schinner blushed to their ears.

"Well, with me," said the artist, "the case is different. It isn't on account of fashion; but I don't want to be recognized. Have the goodness not to betray me, monsieur; I am supposed to be a little painter of no consequence,—a mere decorator. I'm on may way to a chateau where I mustn't rouse the slightest suspicion."

"Ah! I see," said the count, "some intrigue,—a love affair! Youth is happy!"

Oscar, who was writhing in his skin at being a nobody and having nothing to say, gazed at Colonel Czerni-Georges and at the famous painter Schinner, and wondered how he could transform himself into somebody. But a youth of nineteen, kept at home all his life, and going for two weeks only into the country, what could he be, or do, or say? However, the Alicante had got into his head, and his vanity was boiling in his veins; so when the famous Schinner allowed a romantic adventure to be guessed at in which the danger seemed as great as the pleasure, he fastened his eyes, sparkling with wrath and envy, upon that hero.

"Yes," said the count, with a credulous air, "a man must love a woman well to make such sacrifices."

"What sacrifices?" demanded Mistigris.

"Don't you know, my little friend, that a ceiling painted by so great a master as yours is worth its weight in gold?" replied the count. "If the civil list paid you, as it did, thirty thousand francs for each of those rooms in the Louvre," he continued, addressing Schinner, "a bourgeois,—as you call us in the studios—ought certainly to pay you twenty thousand. Whereas, if you go to this chateau as a humble decorator, you will not get two thousand."

"The money is not the greatest loss," said Mistigris. "The work is sure to be a masterpiece, but he can't sign it, you know, for fear of compromising *her*."

"Ah! I'd return all my crosses to the sovereigns who gave them to me for the devotion that youth can win," said the count.

"That's just it!" said Mistigris, "when one's young, one's loved; plenty of love, plenty of women; but they do say: 'Where there's wife, there's mope.'"

"What does Madame Schinner say to all this?" pursued the count; "for I believe you married, out of love, the beautiful Adelaide de Rouville, the protegee of old Admiral de Kergarouet; who, by the bye, obtained for you the order for the Louvre ceilings through his nephew, the Comte de Fontaine."

"A great painter is never married when he travels," said Mistigris.

"So that's the morality of studios, is it?" cried the count, with an air of great simplicity.

"Is the morality of courts where you got those decorations of yours any better?" said Schinner, recovering his self-possession, upset for the moment by finding out how much the count knew of Schinner's life as an artist.

"I never asked for any of my orders," said the count. "I believe I have loyally earned them."

"'A fair yield and no flavor,'" said Mistigris.

The count was resolved not to betray himself; he assumed an air of good-humored interest in the country, and looked up the valley of Groslay as the coucou took the road to Saint-Brice, leaving that to Chantilly on the right.

"Is Rome as fine as they say it is?" said Georges, addressing the great painter.

"Rome is fine only to those who love it; a man must have a passion for it to enjoy it. As a city, I prefer Venice,—though I just missed being murdered there."

"Faith, yes!" cried Mistigris; "if it hadn't been for me you'd have been gobbled up. It was that mischief-making tom-fool, Lord Byron, who got you into the scrape. Oh! wasn't he raging, that buffoon of an Englishman?"

"Hush!" said Schinner. "I don't want my affair with Lord Byron talked about."

"But you must own, all the same, that you were glad enough I knew how to box," said Mistigris.

From time to time, Pierrotin exchanged sly glances with the count, which might have made less inexperienced persons than the five other travellers uneasy.

"Lords, pachas, and thirty-thousand-franc ceilings!" he cried. "I seem to be driving sovereigns. What pourboires I'll get!"

"And all the places paid for!" said Mistigris, slyly.

"It is a lucky day for me," continued Pierrotin; "for you know, Pere Leger, about my beautiful new coach on which I have paid an advance of two thousand francs? Well, those dogs of carriage-builders, to whom I have to pay two thousand five hundred francs more, won't take fifteen hundred down, and my note for a thousand for two months! Those vultures want it all. Who ever heard of being so stiff with a man in business these eight years, and the father of a family?—making me run the risk of losing everything, carriage and money too, if I can't find before to-morrow night that miserable last thousand! Hue, Bichette! They won't play that trick on the great coach offices, I'll warrant you."

"Yes, that's it," said the rapin; "'your money or your strife.'"

"Well, you have only eight hundred now to get," remarked the count, who considered this moan, addressed to Pere Leger, a sort of letter of credit drawn upon himself.

"True," said Pierrotin. "Xi! xi! Rougeot!"

"You must have seen many fine ceilings in Venice," resumed the count, addressing Schinner.

"I was too much in love to take any notice of what seemed to me then mere trifles," replied Schinner. "But I was soon cured of that folly, for it was in the Venetian states—in Dalmatia—that I received a cruel lesson."

"Can it be told?" asked Georges. "I know Dalmatia very well."

"Well, if you have been there, you know that all the people at that end of the Adriatic are pirates, rovers, corsairs retired from business, as they haven't been hanged—"

"Uscoques," said Georges.

Hearing the right name given, the count, who had been sent by Napoleon on one occasion to the Illyrian provinces, turned his head and looked at Georges, so surprised was he.

"The affair happened in that town where they make maraschino," continued Schinner, seeming to search for a name.

"Zara," said Georges. "I've been there; it is on the coast."

"You are right," said the painter. "I had gone there to look at the country, for I adore scenery. I've longed a score of times to paint landscape, which no one, as I think, understands but Mistigris, who will some day reproduce Hobbema, Ruysdael, Claude Lorrain, Poussin, and others."

"But," exclaimed the count, "if he reproduces one of them won't that be enough?"

74

"If you persist in interrupting, monsieur," said Oscar, "we shall never get on."

"And Monsieur Schinner was not addressing himself to you in particular," added Georges.

"'Tisn't polite to interrupt," said Mistigris, sententiously, "but we all do it, and conversation would lose a great deal if we didn't scatter little condiments while exchanging our reflections. Therefore, continue, agreeable old gentleman, to lecture us, if you like. It is done in the best society, and you know the proverb: 'we must 'owl with the wolves.'"

"I had heard marvellous things of Dalmatia," resumed Schinner, "so I went there, leaving Mistigris in Venice at an inn—"

"'Locanda,'" interposed Mistigris; "keep to the local color."

"Zara is what is called a country town—"

"Yes," said Georges; "but it is fortified."

"Parbleu!" said Schinner; "the fortifications count for much in my adventure. At Zara there are a great many apothecaries. I lodged with one. In foreign countries everybody makes a principal business of letting lodgings; all other trades are accessory. In the evening, linen changed, I sat in my balcony. In the opposite balcony I saw a woman; oh! such a woman! Greek,—*that tells all!* The most beautiful creature in the town; almond eyes, lids that dropped like curtains, lashes like a paint-brush, a face with an oval to drive Raffaelle mad, a skin of the most delicious coloring, tints well-blended, velvety! and hands, oh!—"

"They weren't made of butter like those of the David school," put in Mistigris.

"You are always lugging in your painting," cried Georges.

"La, la!" retorted Mistigris; "'an ounce o' paint is worth a pound of swagger.'"

"And such a costume! pure Greek!" continued Schinner. "Conflagration of soul! you understand? Well, I questioned my Diafoirus; and he told me that my neighbor was named Zena. Changed my linen. The husband, an old villain, in order to marry Zena, paid three hundred thousand francs to her father and mother, so celebrated was the beauty of that beautiful creature, who was truly the most beautiful girl in all Dalmatia, Illyria, Adriatica, and other places. In those parts they buy their wives without seeing them—"

"I shall not go *there*," said Pere Leger.

"There are nights when my sleep is still illuminated by the eyes of Zena," continued Schinner. "The husband was sixty-nine years of age, and jealous! not as a tiger, for they say of a tiger, 'jealous as a Dalmatian'; and my man was worse than A Dalmatian, one Dalmatian,—he was three and a half Dalmatians at the very least; he was an Uscoque, tricoque, archicoque in a bicoque of a paltry little place like Zara—"

"Horrid fellow, and 'horrider bellow,'" put in Mistigris.

"Ha! good," said Georges, laughing.

"After being a corsair, and probably a pirate, he thought no more of spitting a Christian on his dagger than I did of spitting on the ground," continued Schinner. "So that was how the land lay. The old wretch had millions, and was hideous with the loss of an ear some pacha had cut off, and the want of an eye left I don't know where. 'Never,' said the little Diafoirus, 'never does he leave his wife, never for a second.' 'Perhaps she'll want your services, and I could go in your clothes; that's a trick that has great success in our theatres,' I told him. Well, it would take too long to tell you all the delicious moments of that lifetime—to wit, three days—which I passed exchanging looks with Zena, and changing linen every day. It was all the more violently titillating because the slightest motion was significant and dangerous. At last it must have dawned upon Zena's mind that none but a Frenchman and an artist was daring enough to make eyes at her in the midst of the perils by which she was surrounded; and as she hated her hideous pirate, she answered my glances with delightful ogles fit to raise a man to the summit of Paradise without pulleys. I attained to the height of Don Quixote; I rose to exaltation! and I cried: 'The monster may kill me, but I'll go, I'll go!' I gave up landscape and studied the ignoble dwelling of the Uscoque. That night, changed linen, and put on the most perfumed shirt I had; then I crossed the street, and entered—"

"The house?" cried Oscar.

"The house?" echoed Georges.

"The house," said Schinner.

"Well, you're a bold dog," cried farmer Leger. "I should have kept out of it myself."

"Especially as you could never have got through the doorway," replied Schinner. "So in I went," he resumed, "and I found two hands stretched out to meet mine. I said nothing, for those hands, soft as the peel of an onion, enjoined me to silence. A whisper breathed into my ear, 'He sleeps!' Then, as we were sure that nobody would see us, we went to walk, Zena and I, upon the ramparts, but accompanied, if you please, by a duenna, as hideous as an old portress, who didn't leave us any more than our shadow; and I couldn't persuade Madame Pirate to send her away. The next night we did the same thing, and again I wanted to get rid of the old woman, but Zena resisted. As my sweet love spoke only Greek, and I Venetian, we couldn't understand each other, and so we quarrelled. I said to myself, in changing linen, 'As sure as fate, the next time there'll be no old woman, and we can make it all up with the language of love.' Instead of which, fate willed that that old woman should save my life! You'll hear how. The weather was fine, and, not to create suspicion, I took a turn at landscape,—this was after our quarrel was made up, you understand. After walking along the ramparts for some time, I was coming tranquilly home with my hands in my pockets, when I saw the street crowded with people. Such a crowd! like that for an execution. It fell upon me; I was seized, garroted, gagged, and guarded by the police. Ah! you don't know—and I hope you never may know—what it is to be taken for a murderer by a maddened populace which stones you and howls after you from end to end of the principal street of a town, shouting for your death! Ah! those eyes were so many flames, all mouths were a single curse, while from the volume of that burning hatred rose the fearful cry: 'To death! to death! down with the murderer!'"

"So those Dalmatians spoke our language, did they?" said the count. "I observe you relate the scene as if it happened yesterday."

Schinner was nonplussed.

"Riot has but one language," said the astute statesman Mistigris.

"Well," continued Schinner, "when I was brought into court in presence of the magistrates, I learned that the cursed corsair was dead, poisoned by Zena. I'd liked to have changed linen then. Give you my word, I knew nothing of *that* melodrama. It seems the Greek girl put opium (a great many poppies, as monsieur told us, grow about there) in the pirate's grog, just to make him sleep soundly and leave her free for a little walk with me, and the old duenna, unfortunate creature, made a mistake and trebled the dose. The immense fortune of that cursed pirate was really the cause of all my Zena's troubles. But she explained matters so ingenuously that I, for one, was released with an injunction from the mayor and the Austrian commissary of police to go back to Rome. Zena, who let the heirs of the Uscoque and the judges get most of the old villain's wealth, was let off with two years' seclusion in a convent, where she still is. I am going back there some day to paint her portrait; for in a few years, you know, all this will be forgotten. Such are the follies one commits at eighteen!"

"And you left me without a sou in the locanda at Venice," said Mistigris. "And I had to get from Venice to Rome by painting portraits for five francs apiece, which they didn't pay me. However, that was my halcyon time. I don't regret it."

"You can imagine the reflections that came to me in that Dalmatian prison, thrown there without protection, having to answer to Austrians and Dalmatians, and in danger of losing my head because I went twice to walk with a woman. There's ill-luck, with a vengeance!"

"Did all that really happen to you?" said Oscar, naively.

"Why shouldn't it happen to him, inasmuch as it had already happened during the French occupation of Illyria to one of our most gallant officers of artillery?" said the count, slyly.

"And you believed that artillery officer?" said Mistigris, as slyly to the count.

"Is that all?" asked Oscar.

"Of course he can't tell you that they cut his head off,—how could he?" said Mistigris. "'Dead schinners tell no tales.'"

"Monsieur, are there farms in that country?" asked Pere Leger. "What do they cultivate?"

"Maraschino," replied Mistigris,—"a plant that grows to the height of the lips, and produces a liqueur which goes by that name."

"Ah!" said Pere Leger.

"I only stayed three days in the town and fifteen in prison," said Schinner, "so I saw nothing; not even the fields where they grow the maraschino."

"They are fooling you," said Georges to the farmer. "Maraschino comes in cases."

"'Romances alter cases,'" remarked Mistigris.

# CHAPTER V

## THE DRAMA BEGINS

Pierrotin's vehicle was now going down the steep incline of the valley of Saint-Brice to the inn which stands in the middle of the large village of that name, where Pierrotin was in the habit of stopping an hour to breathe his horses, give them their oats, and water them. It was now about half-past one o'clock.

"Ha! here's Pere Leger," cried the inn-keeper, when the coach pulled up before the door. "Do you breakfast?"

"Always once a day," said the fat farmer; "and I'll break a crust here and now."

"Give us a good breakfast," cried Georges, twirling his cane in a cavalier manner which excited the admiration of poor Oscar.

But that admiration was turned to jealousy when he saw the gay adventurer pull out from a side-pocket a small straw case, from which he selected a light-colored cigar, which he proceeded to smoke on the threshold of the inn door while waiting for breakfast.

"Do you smoke?" he asked of Oscar.

"Sometimes," replied the ex-schoolboy, swelling out his little chest and assuming a jaunty air.

Georges presented the open case to Oscar and Schinner.

"Phew!" said the great painter; "ten-sous cigars!"

"The remains of those I brought back from Spain," said the adventurer. "Do you breakfast here?"

"No," said the artist. "I am expected at the chateau. Besides, I took something at the Lion d'Argent just before starting."

"And you?" said Georges to Oscar.

"I have breakfasted," replied Oscar.

Oscar would have given ten years of his life for boots and straps to his trousers. He sneezed, he coughed, he spat, and swallowed the smoke with ill-disguised grimaces.

"You don't know how to smoke," said Schinner; "look at me!"

With a motionless face Schinner breathed in the smoke of his cigar and let it out through his nose without the slightest contraction of feature. Then he took another whiff, kept the smoke in his throat, removed the cigar from his lips, and allowed the smoke slowly and gracefully to escape them.

"There, young man," said the great painter.

"Here, young man, here's another way; watch this," said Georges, imitating Schinner, but swallowing the smoke and exhaling none.

"And my parents believed they had educated me!" thought Oscar, endeavoring to smoke with better grace.

But his nausea was so strong that he was thankful when Mistigris filched his cigar, remarking, as he smoked it with evident satisfaction, "You haven't any contagious diseases, I hope."

Oscar in reply would fain have punched his head.

"How he does spend money!" he said, looking at Colonel Georges. "Eight francs for Alicante and the cheese-cakes; forty sous for cigars; and his breakfast will cost him—"

"Ten francs at least," replied Mistigris; "but that's how things are. 'Sharp stomachs make short purses.'"

"Come, Pere Leger, let us drink a bottle of Bordeaux together," said Georges to the farmer.

"Twenty francs for his breakfast!" cried Oscar; "in all, more than thirty-odd francs since we started!"

Killed by a sense of his inferiority, Oscar sat down on a stone post, lost in a revery which did not allow him to perceive that his trousers, drawn up by the effect of his position, showed the point of junction between the old top of his stocking and the new "footing,"—his mother's handiwork.

"We are brothers in socks," said Mistigris, pulling up his own trousers sufficiently to show an effect of the same kind,—"'By the footing, Hercules.'"

The count, who overheard this, laughed as he stood with folded arms under the porte-cochere, a little behind the other travellers. However nonsensical these lads might be, the grave statesman envied their very follies; he liked their bragging and enjoyed the fun of their lively chatter.

"Well, are you to have Les Moulineaux? for I know you went to Paris to get the money for the purchase," said the inn-keeper to Pere Leger, whom he had just taken to the stables to see a horse he wanted to sell to him. "It will be queer if you manage to fleece a peer of France and a minister of State like the Comte de Serizy."

The person thus alluded to showed no sign upon his face as he turned to look at the farmer.

"I've done for him," replied Pere Leger, in a low voice.

"Good! I like to see those nobles fooled. If you should want twenty thousand francs or so, I'll lend them to you—But Francois, the conductor of Touchard's six o'clock coach, told me that Monsieur Margueron was invited by the Comte de Serizy to dine with him to-day at Presles."

"That was the plan of his Excellency, but we had our own little ways of thwarting it," said the farmer, laughing.

"The count could appoint Monsieur Margueron's son, and you haven't any place to give,—remember that," said the inn-keeper.

"Of course I do; but if the count has the ministry on his side, I have King Louis XVIII.," said Pere Leger, in a low voice. "Forty thousand of his pictures on coin of the realm given to Moreau will enable me to buy Les Moulineaux for two hundred and sixty thousand, money down, before Monsieur de Serizy can do so. When he finds the sale is made, he'll be glad enough to buy the farm for three hundred and sixty thousand, instead of letting me cut it up in small lots right in the heart of his property."

"Well done, bourgeois!" cried the inn-keeper.

"Don't you think that's good play?" said Leger.

"Besides," said the inn-keeper, "the farm is really worth that to him."

"Yes; Les Moulineaux brings in to-day six thousand francs in rental. I'll take another lease of it at seven thousand five hundred for eighteen years. Therefore it is really an investment at more than two and a half per cent. The count can't complain of that. In order not to involve Moreau, he is himself to propose me as tenant and farmer; it gives him a look of acting for his master's interests by finding him nearly three per cent for his money, and a tenant who will pay well."

"How much will Moreau make, in all?"

"Well, if the count gives him ten thousand francs for the transaction the matter will bring him fifty thousand,—and well-earned, too."

"After all, the count, so they tell me, doesn't like Presles. And then he is so rich, what does it matter what it costs him?" said the inn-keeper. "I have never seen him, myself."

"Nor I," said Pere Leger. "But he must be intending to live there, or why should he spend two hundred thousand francs in restoring the chateau? It is as fine now as the King's own palace."

"Well, well," said the inn-keeper, "it was high time for Moreau to feather his nest."

"Yes, for if the masters come there," replied Leger, "they won't keep their eyes in their pockets."

The count lost not a word of this conversation, which was held in a low voice, but not in a whisper.

"Here I have actually found the proofs I was going down there to seek," he thought, looking at the fat farmer as he entered the kitchen. "But perhaps," he added, "it is only a scheme; Moreau may not have listened to it."

So unwilling was he to believe that his steward could lend himself to such a conspiracy.

Pierrotin here came out to water his horses. The count, thinking that the driver would probably breakfast with the farmer and the inn-keeper, feared some thoughtless indiscretion.

"All these people combine against us," he thought; "it is allowable to baffle them—Pierrotin," he said in a low voice as the man passed him, "I promised you ten louis to keep my secret; but if you continue to conceal my name (and remember, I shall know if you pronounce it, or make the slightest sign that reveals it to any one, no matter who, here or at Isle-Adam, before to-night), I will give you to-morrow morning, on your return trip, the thousand francs you need to pay for your new coach. Therefore, by way of precaution," added the count, striking Pierrotin, who was pale with happiness, on the shoulder, "don't go in there to breakfast; stay with your horses."

"Monsieur le comte, I understand you; don't be afraid! it relates to Pere Leger, of course."

"It relates to every one," replied the count.

"Make yourself easy.—Come, hurry," said Pierrotin, a few moments later, putting his head into the kitchen. "We are late. Pere Leger, you know there's a hill to climb; I'm not hungry, and I'll drive on slowly; you can soon overtake me,—it will do you good to walk a bit."

"What a hurry you are in, Pierrotin!" said the inn-keeper. "Can't you stay and breakfast? The colonel here pays for the wine at fifty sous, and has ordered a bottle of champagne."

"I can't. I've got a fish I must deliver by three o'clock for a great dinner at Stors; there's no fooling with customers, or fishes, either."

"Very good," said Pere Leger to the inn-keeper. "You can harness that horse you want to sell me into the cabriolet; we'll breakfast in peace and overtake Pierrotin, and I can judge of the beast as we go along. We can go three in your jolter."

To the count's surprise, Pierrotin himself rebridled the horses. Schinner and Mistigris had walked on. Scarcely had Pierrotin overtaken the two artists and was mounting the hill from which Ecouen, the steeple of Mesnil, and the forests that surround that most beautiful region, came in sight, when the gallop of a horse and the jingling of a vehicle announced the coming of Pere Leger and the grandson of Czerni-Georges, who were soon restored to their places in the coucou.

As Pierrotin drove down the narrow road to Moisselles, Georges, who had so far not ceased to talk with the farmer of the beauty of the hostess at Saint-Brice, suddenly exclaimed: "Upon my word, this landscape is not so bad, great painter, is it?"

"Pooh! you who have seen the East and Spain can't really admire it."

"I've two cigars left! If no one objects, will you help me finish them, Schinner? the little young man there seems to have found a whiff or two enough for him."

Pere Leger and the count kept silence, which passed for consent.

Oscar, furious at being called a "little young man," remarked, as the other two were lighting their cigars:

"I am not the aide-de-camp of Mina, monsieur, and I have not yet been to the East, but I shall probably go there. The career to which my family destine me will spare me, I trust, the annoyances of travelling in a coucou before I reach your present age. When I once become a personage I shall know how to maintain my station."

"'Et caetera punctum!'" crowed Mistigris, imitating the hoarse voice of a young cock; which made Oscar's deliverance all the more absurd, because he had just reached the age when the beard sprouts and the voice breaks. "'What a chit for chat!'" added the rapin.

"Your family, young man, destine you to some career, do they?" said Georges. "Might I ask what it is?"

"Diplomacy," replied Oscar.

Three bursts of laughter came from Mistigris, the great painter, and the farmer. The count himself could not help smiling. Georges was perfectly grave.

"By Allah!" he exclaimed, "I see nothing to laugh at in that. Though it seems to me, young man, that your respectable mother is, at the present moment, not exactly in the social sphere of an ambassadress. She carried a handbag worthy of the utmost respect, and wore shoe-strings which—"

"My mother, monsieur!" exclaimed Oscar, in a tone of indignation. "That was the person in charge of our household."

"'Our household' is a very aristocratic term," remarked the count.

"Kings have households," replied Oscar, proudly.

A look from Georges repressed the desire to laugh which took possession of everybody; he contrived to make Mistigris and the painter understand that it was necessary to manage Oscar cleverly in order to work this new mine of amusement.

"Monsieur is right," said the great Schinner to the count, motioning towards Oscar. "Well-bred people always talk of their 'households'; it is only common persons like ourselves who say 'home.' For a man so covered with decorations—"

"'Nunc my eye, nunc alii,'" whispered Mistigris.

"—you seem to know little of the language of the courts. I ask your future protection, Excellency," added Schinner, turning to Oscar.

"I congratulate myself on having travelled with three such distinguished men," said the count,—"a painter already famous, a future general, and a young diplomatist who may some day recover Belgium for France."

Having committed the odious crime of repudiating his mother, Oscar, furious from a sense that his companions were laughing at him, now resolved, at any cost, to make them pay attention to him.

"'All is not gold that glitters,'" he began, his eyes flaming.

"That's not it," said Mistigris. "'All is not old that titters.' You'll never get on in diplomacy if you don't know your proverbs better than that."

"I may not know proverbs, but I know my way—"

"It must be far," said Georges, "for I saw that person in charge of your household give you provisions enough for an ocean voyage: rolls, chocolate—"

"A special kind of bread and chocolate, yes, monsieur," returned Oscar; "my stomach is much too delicate to digest the victuals of a tavern."

"'Victuals' is a word as delicate and refined as your stomach," said Georges.

"Ah! I like that word 'victuals,'" cried the great painter.

"The word is all the fashion in the best society," said Mistigris. "I use it myself at the cafe of the Black Hen."

"Your tutor is, doubtless, some celebrated professor, isn't he?— Monsieur Andrieux of the Academie Francaise, or Monsieur Royer-Collard?" asked Schinner.

"My tutor is or was the Abbe Loraux, now vicar of Saint-Sulpice," replied Oscar, recollecting the name of the confessor at his school.

"Well, you were right to take a private tutor," said Mistigris. "'Tuto, tutor, celeritus, and jocund.' Of course, you will reward him well, your abbe?"

"Undoubtedly he will be made a bishop some day," said Oscar.

"By your family influence?" inquired Georges gravely.

"We shall probably contribute to his rise, for the Abbe Frayssinous is constantly at our house."

"Ah! you know the Abbe Frayssinous?" asked the count.

"He is under obligations to my father," answered Oscar.

"Are you on your way to your estate?" asked Georges.

"No, monsieur; but I am able to say where I am going, if others are not. I am going to the Chateau de Presles, to the Comte de Serizy."

"The devil! are you going to Presles?" cried Schinner, turning as red as a cherry.

"So you know his Excellency the Comte de Serizy?" said Georges.

Pere Leger turned round to look at Oscar with a stupefied air.

"Is Monsieur de Serizy at Presles?" he said.

"Apparently, as I am going there," replied Oscar.

"Do you often see the count," asked Monsieur de Serizy.

"Often," replied Oscar. "I am a comrade of his son, who is about my age, nineteen; we ride together on horseback nearly every day."

"'Aut Caesar, aut Serizy,'" said Mistigris, sententiously.

Pierrotin and Pere Leger exchanged winks on hearing this statement.

"Really," said the count to Oscar, "I am delighted to meet with a young man who can tell me about that personage. I want his influence on a rather serious matter, although it would cost him nothing to oblige me. It concerns a claim I wish to press on the American government. I should be glad to obtain information about Monsieur de Serizy."

"Oh! if you want to succeed," replied Oscar, with a knowing look, "don't go to him, but go to his wife; he is madly in love with her; no one knows more than I do about that; but she can't endure him."

"Why not?" said Georges.

"The count has a skin disease which makes him hideous. Doctor Albert has tried in vain to cure it. The count would give half his fortune if he had a chest like mine," said Oscar, swelling himself out. "He lives a lonely life in his own house; gets up very early in the morning and works from three to eight o'clock; after eight he takes his remedies,—sulphur-baths, steam-baths, and such things. His valet bakes him in a sort of iron box—for he is always in hopes of getting cured."

"If he is such a friend of the King as they say he is, why doesn't he get his Majesty to touch him?" asked Georges.

"The count has lately promised thirty thousand francs to a celebrated Scotch doctor who is coming over to treat him," continued Oscar.

"Then his wife can't be blamed if she finds better—" said Schinner, but he did not finish his sentence.

"I should say so!" resumed Oscar. "The poor man is so shrivelled and old you would take him for eighty! He's as dry as parchment, and, unluckily for him, he feels his position."

"Most men would," said Pere Leger.

"He adores his wife and dares not find fault with her," pursued Oscar, rejoicing to have found a topic to which they listened. "He plays scenes with her which would make you die of laughing,—exactly like Arnolphe in Moliere's comedy."

The count, horror-stricken, looked at Pierrotin, who, finding that the count said nothing, concluded that Madame Clapart's son was telling falsehoods.

"So, monsieur," continued Oscar, "if you want the count's influence, I advise you to apply to the Marquis d'Aiglemont. If you get that former adorer of Madame de Serizy on your side, you will win husband and wife at one stroke."

"Look here!" said the painter, "you seem to have seen the count without his clothes; are you his valet?"

"His valet!" cried Oscar.

"Hang it! people don't tell such things about their friends in public conveyances," exclaimed Mistigris. "As for me, I'm not listening to you; I'm deaf: 'discretion plays the better part of adder.'"

"'A poet is nasty and not fit,' and so is a tale-bearer," cried Schinner.

"Great painter," said Georges, sententiously, "learn this: you can't say harm of people you don't know. Now the little one here has proved, indubitably, that he knows his Serizy by heart. If he had told us about the countess, perhaps—?"

"Stop! not a word about the Comtesse de Serizy, young men," cried the count. "I am a friend of her brother, the Marquis de Ronquerolles, and whoever attempts to speak disparagingly of the countess must answer to me."

"Monsieur is right," cried the painter; "no man should blaguer women."

"God, Honor, and the Ladies! I believe in that melodrama," said Mistigris.

"I don't know the guerrilla chieftain, Mina, but I know the Keeper of the Seals," continued the count, looking at Georges; "and though I don't wear my decorations," he added, looking at the painter, "I prevent those who do not deserve them from obtaining any. And finally, let me say that I know so many persons that I even know Monsieur Grindot, the architect of Presles. Pierrotin, stop at the next inn; I want to get out a moment."

Pierrotin hurried his horses through the village street of Moisselles, at the end of which was the inn where all travellers stopped. This short distance was done in silence.

"Where is that young fool going?" asked the count, drawing Pierrotin into the inn-yard.

"To your steward. He is the son of a poor lady who lives in the rue de la Cerisaie, to whom I often carry fruit, and game, and poultry from Presles. She is a Madame Husson."

"Who is that man?" inquired Pere Leger of Pierrotin when the count had left him.

"Faith, I don't know," replied Pierrotin; "this is the first time I have driven him. I shouldn't be surprised if he was that prince who owns Maffliers. He has just told me to leave him on the road near there; he doesn't want to go on to Isle-Adam."

"Pierrotin thinks he is the master of Maffliers," said Pere Leger, addressing Georges when he got back into the coach.

The three young fellows were now as dull as thieves caught in the act; they dared not look at each other, and were evidently considering the consequences of their fibs.

"This is what is called 'suffering for license sake,'" said Mistigris.

"You see I did know the count," said Oscar.

90

"Possibly. But you'll never be an ambassador," replied Georges. "When people want to talk in public conveyances, they ought to be careful, like me, to talk without saying anything."

"That's what speech is for," remarked Mistigris, by way of conclusion.

The count returned to his seat and the coucou rolled on amid the deepest silence.

"Well, my friends," said the count, when they reached the Carreau woods, "here we all are, as silent as if we were going to the scaffold."

"'Silence gives content,'" muttered Mistigris.

"The weather is fine," said Georges.

"What place is that?" said Oscar, pointing to the chateau de Franconville, which produces a fine effect at that particular spot, backed, as it is, by the noble forest of Saint-Martin.

"How is it," cried the count, "that you, who say you go so often to Presles, do not know Franconville?"

"Monsieur knows men, not castles," said Mistigris.

"Budding diplomatists have so much else to take their minds," remarked Georges.

"Be so good as to remember my name," replied Oscar, furious. "I am Oscar Husson, and ten years hence I shall be famous."

After that speech, uttered with bombastic assumption, Oscar flung himself back in his corner.

"Husson of what, of where?" asked Mistigris.

"It is a great family," replied the count. "Husson de la Cerisaie; monsieur was born beneath the steps of the Imperial throne."

Oscar colored crimson to the roots of his hair, and was penetrated through and through with a dreadful foreboding.

They were now about to descend the steep hill of La Cave, at the foot of which, in a narrow valley, flanked by the forest of Saint-Martin, stands the magnificent chateau of Presles.

"Messieurs," said the count, "I wish you every good fortune in your various careers. Monsieur le colonel, make your peace with the King of France; the Czerni-Georges ought not to snub the Bourbons. I have nothing to wish for you, my dear Monsieur Schinner; your fame is already won, and nobly won by splendid work. But you are much to be feared in domestic life, and I, being a married man, dare not invite you to my house. As for Monsieur Husson, he needs no protection; he possesses the secrets of statesmen and can make them tremble. Monsieur Leger is about to pluck the Comte de Serizy, and I can only exhort him to do it with a firm hand. Pierrotin, put me out here, and pick me up at the same place to-morrow," added the count, who then left the coach and took a path through the woods, leaving his late companions confused and bewildered.

"He must be that count who has hired Franconville; that's the path to it," said Leger.

"If ever again," said the false Schinner, "I am caught blague-ing in a public coach, I'll fight a duel with myself. It was your fault, Mistigris," giving his rapin a tap on the head.

"All I did was to help you out, and follow you to Venice," said Mistigris; "but that's always the way, 'Fortune belabors the slave.'"

"Let me tell you," said Georges to his neighbor Oscar, "that if, by chance, that was the Comte de Serizy, I wouldn't be in your skin for a good deal, healthy as you think it."

Oscar, remembering his mother's injunctions, which these words recalled to his mind, turned pale and came to his senses.

"Here you are, messieurs!" cried Pierrotin, pulling up at a fine iron gate.

"Here we are—where?" said the painter, and Georges, and Oscar all at once.

"Well, well!" exclaimed Pierrotin, "if that doesn't beat all! Ah ca, monsieurs, have none of you been here before? Why, this is the chateau de Presles."

"Oh, yes; all right, friend," said Georges, recovering his audacity. "But I happen to be going on to Les Moulineaux," he added, not wishing his companions to know that he was really going to the chateau.

"You don't say so? Then you are coming to me," said Pere Leger.

"How so?"

"Why, I'm the farmer at Moulineaux. Hey, colonel, what brings you there?"

"To taste your butter," said Georges, pulling out his portfolio.

"Pierrotin," said Oscar, "leave my things at the steward's. I am going straight to the chateau."

Whereupon Oscar plunged into a narrow path, not knowing, in the least, where he was going.

"Hi! Monsieur l'ambassadeur," cried Pere Leger, "that's the way to the forest; if you really want to get to the chateau, go through the little gate."

Thus compelled to enter, Oscar disappeared into the grand court-yard. While Pere Leger stood watching Oscar, Georges, utterly confounded by the discovery that the farmer was the present occupant of Les Moulineaux, has slipped away so adroitly that when the fat countryman looked round for his colonel there was no sign of him.

The iron gates opened at Pierrotin's demand, and he proudly drove in to deposit with the concierge the thousand and one utensils belonging to the great Schinner. Oscar was thunderstruck when he became aware that Mistigris and his master, the witnesses of his bravado, were to be installed in the chateau itself. In ten minutes Pierrotin had discharged the various packages of the painter, the bundles of Oscar Husson, and the pretty little leather portmanteau, which he took from its nest of hay and confided mysteriously to the wife of the concierge. Then he drove out of the courtyard, cracking his whip, and took the road that led through the forest to Isle-Adam, his face beaming with the sly expression of a peasant who calculates his profits. Nothing was lacking now to his happiness; on the morrow he would have his thousand francs, and, as a consequence, his magnificent new coach.

# CHAPTER VI

## THE MOREAU INTERIOR

Oscar, somewhat abashed, was skulking behind a clump of trees in the centre of the court-yard, and watching to see what became of his two road-companions, when Monsieur Moreau suddenly came out upon the portico from what was called the guard-room. He was dressed in a long blue overcoat which came to his heels, breeches of yellowish leather and top-boots, and in his hand he carried a riding-whip.

"Ah! my boy, so here you are? How is the dear mamma?" he said, taking Oscar by the hand. "Good-day, messieurs," he added to Mistigris and his master, who then came forward. "You are, no doubt, the two painters whom Monsieur Grindot, the architect, told me to expect."

He whistled twice at the end of his whip; the concierge came.

"Take these gentlemen to rooms 14 and 15. Madame Moreau will give you the keys. Go with them to show the way; make fires there, if necessary, and take up all their things. I have orders from Monsieur le comte," he added, addressing the two young men, "to invite you to my table, messieurs; we dine at five, as in Paris. If you like hunting, you will find plenty to amuse you; I have a license from the Eaux et Forets; and we hunt over twelve thousand acres of forest, not counting our own domain."

Oscar, the painter, and Mistigris, all more or less subdued, exchanged glances, but Mistigris, faithful to himself, remarked in a low tone, "'Veni, vidi, cecidi,—I came, I saw, I slaughtered.'"

Oscar followed the steward, who led him along at a rapid pace through the park.

"Jacques," said Moreau to one of his children whom they met, "run in and tell your mother that little Husson has come, and say to her that I am obliged to go to Les Moulineaux for a moment."

The steward, then about fifty years old, was a dark man of medium height, and seemed stern. His bilious complexion, to which country habits had added a certain violent coloring, conveyed, at first sight, the impression of a nature which was other than his own. His blue eyes and a large crow-beaked nose gave him an air that was the more threatening because his eyes were placed too close together. But his large lips, the outline of his face, and the easy good-humor of his manner soon showed that his nature was a kindly one. Abrupt in speech and decided in tone, he impressed Oscar immensely by the force of his penetration, inspired, no doubt, by the affection which he felt for the boy. Trained by his mother to magnify the steward, Oscar had always felt himself very small in Moreau's presence; but on reaching Presles a new sensation came over him, as if he expected some harm from this fatherly figure, his only protector.

"Well, my Oscar, you don't look pleased at getting here," said the steward. "And yet you'll find plenty of amusement; you shall learn to ride on horseback, and shoot, and hunt."

"I don't know any of those things," said Oscar, stupidly.

"But I brought you here to learn them."

"Mamma told me only to stay two weeks because of Madame Moreau."

"Oh! we'll see about that," replied Moreau, rather wounded that his conjugal authority was doubted.

Moreau's youngest son, an active, strapping lad of twelve, here ran up.

"Come," said his father, "take Oscar to your mother."

He himself went rapidly along the shortest path to the gamekeeper's house, which was situated between the park and the forest.

The pavilion, or lodge, in which the count had established his steward, was built a few years before the Revolution. It stood in the centre of a large garden, one wall of which adjoined the court-yard of the stables and offices of the chateau itself. Formerly its chief entrance was on the main road to the village. But after the count's father bought the building, he closed that entrance and united the place with his own property.

The house, built of freestone, in the style of the period of Louis XV. (it is enough to say that its exterior decoration consisted of a stone drapery beneath the windows, as in the colonnades of the Place Louis XV., the flutings of which were stiff and ungainly), had on the ground-floor a fine salon opening into a bedroom, and a dining-room connected with a billiard-room. These rooms, lying parallel to one another, were separated by a staircase, in front of which was a sort of peristyle which formed an entrance-hall, on which the two suits of rooms on either side opened. The kitchen was beneath the dining-room, for the whole building was raised ten steps from the ground level.

By placing her own bedroom on the first floor above the ground-floor, Madame Moreau was able to transform the chamber adjoining the salon into a boudoir. These two rooms were richly furnished with beautiful pieces culled from the rare old furniture of the chateau. The salon, hung with blue and white damask, formerly the curtains of the state-bed, was draped with ample portieres and window curtains lined with white silk. Pictures, evidently from old panels, plant-stands, various pretty articles of modern upholstery, handsome lamps, and a rare old cut-glass chandelier, gave a grandiose appearance to the room. The carpet was a Persian rug. The boudoir, wholly modern, and furnished entirely after Madame Moreau's own taste, was arranged in imitation of a tent, with ropes of blue silk on a gray background. The classic divan was there, of course, with its pillows and footstools. The plant-stands, taken care of by the head-gardener of Presles, rejoiced the eye with their pyramids of bloom. The dining-room and billiard-room were furnished in mahogany.

Around the house the steward's wife had laid out a beautiful garden, carefully cultivated, which opened into the great park. Groups of choice parks hid the offices and stables. To improve the entrance by which visitors came to see her, she had substituted a handsome iron gateway for the shabby railing, which she discarded.

The dependence in which the situation of their dwelling placed the Moreaus, was thus adroitly concealed, and they seemed all the more like rich and independent persons taking care of the property of a friend, because neither the count nor the countess ever came to Presles to take down their pretensions. Moreover, the perquisites granted by Monsieur de Serizy allowed them to live in the midst of that abundance which is the luxury of country life. Milk, eggs, poultry, game, fruits, flowers, forage, vegetables, wood, the steward and his wife used in profusion, buying absolutely nothing but butcher's-meat, wines, and the colonial supplies required by their life of luxury. The poultry-maid baked their bread; and of late years Moreau had paid his butcher with pigs from the farm, after reserving those he needed for his own use.

On one occasion, the countess, always kind and good to her former maid, gave her, as a souvenir perhaps, a little travelling-carriage, the fashion of which was out of date. Moreau had it repainted, and now drove his wife about the country with two good horses which belonged to the farm. Besides these horses, Moreau had his own saddle-horse. He did enough farming on the count's property to keep the horses and maintain his servants. He stacked three hundred tons of excellent hay, but accounted for only one hundred, making use of a vague permission once granted by the count. He kept his poultry-yard, pigeon-cotes, and cattle at the cost of the estate, but the manure of the stables was used by the count's gardeners. All these little stealings had some ostensible excuse.

Madame Moreau had taken into her service a daughter of one of the gardeners, who was first her maid and afterwards her cook. The poultry-game, also the dairy-maid, assisted in the work of the household; and the steward had hired a discharged soldier to groom the horses and do the heavy labor.

At Nerville, Chaumont, Maffliers, Nointel, and other places of the neighborhood, the handsome wife of the steward was received by persons who either did not know, or pretended not to know her previous condition. Moreau did services to many persons. He induced his master to agree to certain things which seem trifles in Paris, but are really of immense importance in the country. After bringing about the appointment of a certain "juge de paix" at Beaumont and also at Isle-Adam, he had, in the same year, prevented the dismissal of a keeper-general of the Forests, and obtained the cross of the Legion of honor for the first cavalry-sergeant at Beaumont. Consequently, no festivity was ever given among the bourgeoisie to which Monsieur and Madame Moreau were not invited. The rector of Presles and the mayor of Presles came every evening to play cards with them. It is difficult for a man not to be kind and hospitable after feathering his nest so comfortably.

A pretty woman, and an affected one, as all retired waiting-maids of great ladies are, for after they are married they imitate their mistresses, Madame Moreau imported from Paris all the new fashions. She wore expensive boots, and never was seen on foot, except, occasionally, in the finest weather. Though her husband allowed but five hundred francs a year for her toilet, that sum is immense in the provinces, especially if well laid out. So that Madame Moreau, fair, rosy, and fresh, about thirty-six years of age, still slender and delicate in shape in spite of her three children, played the young girl and gave herself the airs of a princess. If, when she drove by in her caleche, some stranger had asked, "Who is she?" Madame Moreau would have been furious had she heard the reply: "The wife of the steward at Presles." She wished to be taken for the mistress of the chateau. In the villages, she patronized the people in the tone of a great lady. The influence of her husband over the count, proved in so many years, prevented the small bourgeoisie from laughing at Madame Moreau, who, in the eyes of the peasants, was really a personage.

Estelle (her name was Estelle) took no more part in the affairs of the stewardship then the wife of a broker does in her husband's affairs at the Bourse. She even depended on Moreau for the care of the household and their own fortune. Confident of his *means*, she was a thousand leagues from dreaming that this comfortable existence, which had lasted for seventeen years, could ever be endangered. And yet, when she heard of the count's determination to restore the magnificent chateau, she felt that her enjoyments were threatened, and she urged her husband to come to the arrangement with Leger about Les Moulineaux, so that they might retire from Presles and live at Isle-Adam. She had no intention of returning to a position that was more or less that of a servant in presence of her former mistress, who, indeed, would have laughed to see her established in the lodge with all the airs and graces of a woman of the world.

The rancorous enmity which existed between the Reyberts and the Moreaus came from a wound inflicted by Madame de Reybert upon Madame Moreau on the first occasion when the latter assumed precedence over the former on her first arrival at Presles, the wife of the steward being determined not to allow her supremacy to be undermined by a woman nee de Corroy. Madame de Reybert thereupon reminded, or, perhaps, informed the whole country-side of Madame Moreau's former station. The words "waiting-maid" flew from lip to lip. The envious acquaintances of the Moreaus throughout the neighborhood from Beaumont to Moisselles, began to carp and criticize with such eagerness that a few sparks of the conflagration fell into the Moreau household. For four years the Reyberts, cut dead by the handsome Estelle, found themselves the objects of so much animadversion on the part of the adherents of the Moreaus that their position at Presles would not have been endurable without the thought of vengeance which had, so far, supported them.

The Moreaus, who were very friendly with Grindot the architect, had received notice from him of the early arrival of the two painters sent down to finish the decorations of the chateau, the principal paintings for which were just completed by Schinner. The great painter had recommended for this work the artist who was accompanied by Mistigris. For two days past Madame Moreau had been on the tiptoe of expectation, and had put herself under arms to receive him. An artist, who was to be her guest and companion for weeks, demanded some effort. Schinner and his wife had their own apartment at the chateau, where, by the count's express orders, they were treated with all the consideration due to himself. Grindot, who stayed at the steward's house, showed such respect for the great artist that neither the steward nor his wife had attempted to put themselves on familiar terms with him. Moreover, the noblest and richest people in the surrounding country had vied with each other in paying attention to Schinner and his wife. So, very well pleased to have, as it were, a little revenge of her own, Madame Moreau was determined to cry up the artist she was now expecting, and to present him to her social circle as equal in talent to the great Schinner.

Though for two days past Moreau's pretty wife had arrayed herself coquettishly, the prettiest of her toilets had been reserved for this very Saturday, when, as she felt no doubt, the artist would arrive for dinner. A pink gown in very narrow stripes, a pink belt with a richly chased gold buckle, a velvet ribbon and cross at her throat, and velvet bracelets on her bare arms (Madame de Serizy had handsome arms and showed them much), together with bronze kid shoes and thread stockings, gave Madame Moreau all the appearance of an elegant Parisian. She wore, also, a superb bonnet of Leghorn straw, trimmed with a bunch of moss roses from Nattier's, beneath the spreading sides of which rippled the curls of her beautiful blond hair.

After ordering a very choice dinner and reviewing the condition of her rooms, she walked about the grounds, so as to be seen standing near a flower-bed in the court-yard of the chateau, like the mistress of the house, on the arrival of the coach from Paris. She held above her head a charming rose-colored parasol lined with white silk and fringed. Seeing that Pierrotin merely left Mistigris's queer packages with the concierge, having, apparently, brought no passengers, Estelle retired disappointed and regretting the trouble of making her useless toilet. Like many persons who are dressed in their best, she felt incapable of any other occupation than that of sitting idly in her salon awaiting the coach from Beaumont, which usually passed about an hour after that of Pierrotin, though it did not leave Paris till mid-day. She was, therefore, in her own apartment when the two artists walked up to the chateau, and were sent by Moreau himself to their rooms where they made their regulation toilet for dinner. The pair had asked questions of their guide, the gardener, who told them so much of Moreau's beauty that they felt the necessity of "rigging themselves up" (studio slang). They, therefore, put on their most superlative suits and then walked over to the steward's lodge, piloted by Jacques Moreau, the eldest son, a hardy youth, dressed like an English boy in a handsome jacket with a turned-over collar, who was spending his vacation like a fish in water on the estate where his father and mother reigned as aristocrats.

"Mamma," he said, "here are the two artists sent down by Monsieur Schinner."

Madame Moreau, agreeably surprised, rose, told her son to place chairs, and began to display her graces.

"Mamma, the Husson boy is with papa," added the lad; "shall I fetch him?"

"You need not hurry; go and play with him," said his mother.

The remark "you need not hurry" proved to the two artists the unimportance of their late travelling companion in the eyes of their hostess; but it also showed, what they did not know, the feeling of a step-mother against a step-son. Madame Moreau, after seventeen years of married life, could not be ignorant of the steward's attachment to Madame Clapart and the little Husson, and she hated both mother and child so vehemently that it is not surprising that Moreau had never before risked bringing Oscar to Presles.

"We are requested, my husband and myself," she said to the two artists, "to do you the honors of the chateau. We both love art, and, above all, artists," she added in a mincing tone; "and I beg you to make yourselves at home here. In the country, you know, every one should be at their ease; one must feel wholly at liberty, or life is *too* insipid. We have already had Monsieur Schinner with us."

Mistigris gave a sly glance at his companion.

"You know him, of course?" continued Estelle, after a slight pause.

"Who does not know him, madame?" said the painter.

"Knows him like his double," remarked Mistigris.

"Monsieur Grindot told me your name," said Madame Moreau to the painter. "But—"

"Joseph Bridau," he replied, wondering with what sort of woman he had to do.

Mistigris began to rebel internally against the patronizing manner of the steward's wife; but he waited, like Bridau, for some word which might give him his cue; one of those words "de singe a dauphin" which artists, cruel, born-observers of the ridiculous—the pabulum of their pencils—seize with such avidity. Meantime Estelle's clumsy hands and feet struck their eyes, and presently a word, or phrase or two, betrayed her past, and quite out of keeping with the elegance of her dress, made the two young fellows aware of their prey. A single glance at each other was enough to arrange a scheme that they should take Estelle seriously on her own ground, and thus find amusement enough during the time of their stay.

"You say you love art, madame; perhaps you cultivate it successfully," said Joseph Bridau.

"No. Without being neglected, my education was purely commercial; but I have so profound and delicate a sense of art that Monsieur Schinner always asked me, when he had finished a piece of work, to give him my opinion on it."

"Just as Moliere consulted La Foret," said Mistigris.

Not knowing that La Foret was Moliere's servant-woman, Madame Moreau inclined her head graciously, showing that in her ignorance she accepted the speech as a compliment.

"Didn't he propose to 'croquer' you?" asked Bridau. "Painters are eager enough after handsome women."

"What may you mean by such language?"

"In the studios we say croquer, craunch, nibble, for sketching," interposed Mistigris, with an insinuating air, "and we are always wanting to croquer beautiful heads. That's the origin of the expression, 'She is pretty enough to eat.'"

"I was not aware of the origin of the term," she replied, with the sweetest glance at Mistigris.

"My pupil here," said Bridau, "Monsieur Leon de Lora, shows a remarkable talent for portraiture. He would be too happy, I know, to leave you a souvenir of our stay by painting your charming head, madame."

Joseph Bridau made a sign to Mistigris which meant: "Come, sail in, and push the matter; she is not so bad in looks, this woman."

Accepting the glance, Leon de Lora slid down upon the sofa beside Estelle and took her hand, which she permitted.

"Oh! madame, if you would like to offer a surprise to your husband, and will give me a few secret sittings I would endeavor to surpass myself. You are so beautiful, so fresh, so charming! A man without any talent might become a genius in painting you. He would draw from your eyes—"

"We must paint your dear children in the arabesques," said Bridau, interrupting Mistigris.

"I would rather have them in the salon; but perhaps I am indiscreet in asking it," she replied, looking at Bridau coquettishly.

"Beauty, madame, is a sovereign whom all painters worship; it has unlimited claims upon them."

"They are both charming," thought Madame Moreau. "Do you enjoy driving? Shall I take you through the woods, after dinner, in my carriage?"

"Oh! oh! oh!" cried Mistigris, in three ecstatic tones. "Why, Presles will prove our terrestrial paradise."

"With an Eve, a fair, young, fascinating woman," added Bridau.

Just as Madame Moreau was bridling, and soaring to the seventh heaven, she was recalled like a kite by a twitch at its line.

"Madame!" cried her maid-servant, bursting into the room.

"Rosalie," said her mistress, "who allowed you to come here without being sent for?"

Rosalie paid no heed to the rebuke, but whispered in her mistress's ear:—

"The count is at the chateau."

"Has he asked for me?" said the steward's wife.

"No, madame; but he wants his trunk and the key of his apartment."

"Then give them to him," she replied, making an impatient gesture to hide her real trouble.

"Mamma! here's Oscar Husson," said her youngest son, bringing in Oscar, who turned as red as a poppy on seeing the two artists in evening dress.

"Oh! so you have come, my little Oscar," said Estelle, stiffly. "I hope you will now go and dress," she added, after looking at him contemptuously from head to foot. "Your mother, I presume, has not accustomed you to dine in such clothes as those."

"Oh!" cried the cruel Mistigris, "a future diplomatist knows the saying that 'two coats are better than none.'"

"How do you mean, a future diplomatist?" exclaimed Madame Moreau.

Poor Oscar had tears in his eyes as he looked in turn from Joseph to Leon.

"Merely a joke made in travelling," replied Joseph, who wanted to save Oscar's feelings out of pity.

"The boy just wanted to be funny like the rest of us, and he blagued, that's all," said Mistigris.

"Madame," said Rosalie, returning to the door of the salon, "his Excellency has ordered dinner for eight, and wants it served at six o'clock. What are we to do?"

During Estelle's conference with her head-woman the two artists and Oscar looked at each other in consternation; their glances were expressive of terrible apprehension.

"His Excellency! who is he?" said Joseph Bridau.

"Why, Monsieur le Comte de Serizy, of course," replied little Moreau.

"Could it have been the count in the coucou?" said Leon de Lora.

"Oh!" exclaimed Oscar, "the Comte de Serizy always travels in his own carriage with four horses."

"How did the Comte de Serizy get here?" said the painter to Madame Moreau, when she returned, much discomfited, to the salon.

"I am sure I do not know," she said. "I cannot explain to myself this sudden arrival; nor do I know what has brought him—And Moreau not here!"

"His Excellency wishes Monsieur Schinner to come over to the chateau," said the gardener, coming to the door of the salon. "And he begs Monsieur Schinner to give him the pleasure to dine with him; also Monsieur Mistigris."

"Done for!" cried the rapin, laughing. "He whom we took for a bourgeois in the coucou was the count. You may well say: 'Sour are the curses of perversity.'"

Oscar was very nearly changed to a pillar of salt; for, at this revelation, his throat felt saltier than the sea.

"And you, who talked to him about his wife's lovers and his skin diseases!" said Mistigris, turning on Oscar.

"What does he mean?" exclaimed the steward's wife, gazing after the two artists, who went away laughing at the expression of Oscar's face.

Oscar remained dumb, confounded, stupefied, hearing nothing, though Madame Moreau questioned him and shook him violently by his arm, which she caught and squeezed. She gained nothing, however, and was forced to leave him in the salon without an answer, for Rosalie appeared again, to ask for linen and silver, and to beg she would go herself and see that the multiplied orders of the count were executed. All the household, together with the gardeners and the concierge and his wife, were going and coming in a confusion that may readily be imagined. The master had fallen upon his own house like a bombshell.

From the top of the hill near La Cave, where he left the coach, the count had gone, by the path through the woods well-known to him, to the house of his gamekeeper. The keeper was amazed when he saw his real master.

"Is Moreau here?" said the count. "I see his horse."

"No, monseigneur; he means to go to Moulineaux before dinner, and he has left his horse here while he went to the chateau to give a few orders."

"If you value your place," said the count, "you will take that horse and ride at once to Beaumont, where you will deliver to Monsieur Margueron the note that I shall now write."

So saying the count entered the keeper's lodge and wrote a line, folding it in a way impossible to open without detection, and gave it to the man as soon as he saw him in the saddle.

"Not a word to any one," he said, "and as for you, madame," he added to the gamekeeper's wife, "if Moreau comes back for his horse, tell him merely that I have taken it."

The count then crossed the park and entered the court-yard of the chateau through the iron gates. However worn-out a man may be by the wear and tear of public life, by his own emotions, by his own mistakes and disappointments, the soul of any man able to love deeply at the

106

count's age is still young and sensitive to treachery. Monsieur de Serizy had felt such pain at the thought that Moreau had deceived him, that even after hearing the conversation at Saint-Brice he thought him less an accomplice of Leger and the notary than their tool. On the threshold of the inn, and while that conversation was still going on, he thought of pardoning his steward after giving him a good reproof. Strange to say, the dishonesty of his confidential agent occupied his mind as a mere episode from the moment when Oscar revealed his infirmities. Secrets so carefully guarded could only have been revealed by Moreau, who had, no doubt, laughed over the hidden troubles of his benefactor with either Madame de Serizy's former maid or with the Aspasia of the Directory.

As he walked along the wood-path, this peer of France, this statesman, wept as young men weep; he wept his last tears. All human feelings were so cruelly hurt by one stroke that the usually calm man staggered through his park like a wounded deer.

When Moreau arrived at the gamekeeper's lodge and asked for his horse, the keeper's wife replied:—

"Monsieur le comte has just taken it."

"Monsieur le comte!" cried Moreau. "Whom do you mean?"

"Why, the Comte de Serizy, our master," she replied. "He is probably at the chateau by this time," she added, anxious to be rid of the steward, who, unable to understand the meaning of her words, turned back towards the chateau.

But he presently turned again and came back to the lodge, intending to question the woman more closely; for he began to see something serious in this secret arrival, and the apparently strange method of his master's return. But the wife of the gamekeeper, alarmed to find herself caught in a vise between the count and his steward, had locked herself into the house, resolved not to open to any but her husband. Moreau, more and more uneasy, ran rapidly, in spite of his boots and spurs, to the chateau, where he was told that the count was dressing.

"Seven persons invited to dinner!" cried Rosalie as soon as she saw him.

Moreau then went through the offices to his own house. On his way he met the poultry-girl, who was having an altercation with a handsome young man.

"Monsieur le comte particularly told me a colonel, an aide-de-camp of Mina," insisted the girl.

"I am not a colonel," replied Georges.

"But isn't your name Georges?"

"What's all this?" said the steward, intervening.

"Monsieur, my name is Georges Marest; I am the son of a rich wholesale ironmonger in the rue Saint-Martin; I come on business to Monsieur le Comte de Serizy from Maitre Crottat, a notary, whose second clerk I am."

"And I," said the girl, "am telling him that monseigneur said to me: 'There'll come a colonel named Czerni-Georges, aide-de-camp to Mina; he'll come by Pierrotin's coach; if he asks for me show him into the waiting-room.'"

"Evidently," said the clerk, "the count is a traveller who came down with us in Pierrotin's coucou; if it hadn't been for the politeness of a young man he'd have come as a rabbit."

"A rabbit! in Pierrotin's coucou!" exclaimed Moreau and the poultry-girl together.

"I am sure of it, from what this girl is now saying," said Georges.

"How so?" asked the steward.

"Ah! that's the point," cried the clerk. "To hoax the travellers and have a bit of fun I told them a lot of stuff about Egypt and Greece and Spain. As I happened to be wearing spurs I have myself out for a colonel of cavalry: pure nonsense!"

"Tell me," said Moreau, "what did this traveller you take to be Monsieur le comte look like?"

"Face like a brick," said Georges, "hair snow-white, and black eyebrows."

"That is he!"

"Then I'm lost!" exclaimed Georges.

"Why?"

"Oh, I chaffed him about his decorations."

"Pooh! he's a good fellow; you probably amused him. Come at once to the chateau. I'll go in and see his Excellency. Where did you say he left the coach?"

"At the top of the mountain."

"I don't know what to make of it!"

"After all," thought Georges, "though I did blague him, I didn't say anything insulting."

"Why have you come here?" asked the steward.

"I have brought the deed of sale for the farm at Moulineaux, all ready for signature."

"Good heavens!" exclaimed the steward, "I don't understand one word of all this!"

Moreau felt his heart beat painfully when, after giving two raps on his master's door, he heard the words:—

"Is that you, *Monsieur* Moreau?"

"Yes, monseigneur."

"Come in."

The count was now wearing a pair of white trousers and thin boots, a white waistcoat and a black coat on which shone the grand cross of the Legion upon the right breast, and fastened to a buttonhole on the left was the order of the Golden Fleece hanging by a short gold chain. He had arranged his hair himself, and had, no doubt, put himself in full dress to do the honors of Presles to Monsieur Margueron; and, possibly, to impress the good man's mind with a prestige of grandeur.

"Well, monsieur," said the count, who remained seated, leaving Moreau to stand before him. "We have not concluded that purchase from Margueron."

"He asks too much for the farm at the present moment."

"But why is he not coming to dinner as I requested?"

"Monseigneur, he is ill."

"Are you sure?"

"I have just come from there."

"Monsieur," said the count, with a stern air which was really terrible, "what would you do with a man whom you trusted, if, after seeing you dress wounds which you desired to keep secret from all the world, he should reveal your misfortunes and laugh at your malady with a strumpet?"

"I would thrash him for it."

"And if you discovered that he was also betraying your confidence and robbing you?"

"I should endeavor to detect him, and send him to the galleys."

"Monsieur Moreau, listen to me. You have undoubtedly spoken of my infirmities to Madame Clapart; you have laughed at her house, and with her, over my attachment to the Comtesse de Serizy; for her son, little Husson, told a number of circumstances relating to my medical treatment, to travellers by a public conveyance in my presence, and Heaven knows in what language! He dared to calumniate my wife. Besides this, I learned from the lips of Pere Leger himself, who was in the coach, of the plan laid by the notary at Beaumont and by you and by himself in relation to Les Moulineaux. If you have been, as you say, to Monsieur Margueron, it was to tell him to feign illness. He is so little ill that he is coming here to dinner this evening. Now, monsieur, I could pardon you having made two hundred and fifty thousand francs out of your situation in seventeen years,—I can understand that. You might each time have asked me for what you took, and I would have given it to you; but let that pass. You have been, notwithstanding this disloyalty, better than others, as I believe. But that you, who knew my toil for our country, for France, you have seen me giving night after night to the Emperor's service, and working eighteen hours of each twenty-four for months together, you who knew my love for Madame de Serizy,—that you should have gossiped about me before a boy! holding up my secrets and my affections to the ridicule of a Madame Husson!—"

"Monseigneur!"

"It is unpardonable. To injure a man's interest, why, that is nothing; but to stab his heart!—Oh! you do not know what you have done!"

The count put his head in his hands and was silent for some moments.

"I leave you what you have gained," he said after a time, "and I shall forget you. For my sake, for my dignity, and for your honor, we will part decently; for I cannot but remember even now what your father did for mine. You will explain the duties of the stewardship in a proper manner to Monsieur de Reybert, who succeeds you. Be calm, as I am. Give no opportunity for fools to talk. Above all, let there be no recrimination or petty meanness. Though you no longer possess my confidence, endeavor to behave with the decorum of well-bred persons. As for that miserable boy who has wounded me to death, I will not have him sleep at Presles; send him to the inn; I will not answer for my own temper if I see him."

"I do not deserve such gentleness, monseigneur," said Moreau, with tears in his eyes. "Yes, you are right; if I had been utterly dishonest I should now be worth five hundred thousand francs instead of half that sum. I offer to give you an account of my fortune, with all its details. But let me tell you, monseigneur, that in talking of you with Madame Clapart, it was never in derision; but, on the contrary, to deplore your state, and to ask her for certain remedies, not used by physicians, but known to the common people. I spoke of your feelings before the boy, who was in his bed and, as I supposed, asleep (it seems he must have been awake and listening to us), with the utmost affection and respect. Alas! fate wills that indiscretions be punished like crimes. But while accepting the results of your just anger, I wish you to know what actually took place. It was, indeed, from heart to heart that I spoke of you to Madame Clapart. As for my wife, I have never said one word of these things—"

"Enough," said the count, whose conviction was now complete; "we are not children. All is now irrevocable. Put your affairs and mine in order. You can stay in the pavilion until October. Monsieur and Madame de Reybert will lodge for the present in the chateau; endeavor to keep on terms with them, like well-bred persons who hate each other, but still keep up appearances."

The count and Moreau went downstairs; Moreau white as the count's hair, the count himself calm and dignified.

During the time this interview lasted the Beaumont coach, which left Paris at one o'clock, had stopped before the gates of the chateau, and deposited Maitre Crottat, the notary, who was shown, according to the count's orders, into the salon, where he found his clerk, extremely subdued in manner, and the two painters, all three of them painfully self-conscious and embarrassed. Monsieur de Reybert, a man of fifty, with a crabbed expression of face, was also there, accompanied by old Margueron and the notary of Beaumont, who held in his hand a bundle of deeds and other papers.

When these various personages saw the count in evening dress, and wearing his orders, Georges Marest had a slight sensation of colic, Joseph Bridau quivered, but Mistigris, who was conscious of being in his Sunday clothes, and had, moreover, nothing on his conscience, remarked, in a sufficiently loud tone:—

"Well, he looks a great deal better like that."

"Little scamp," said the count, catching him by the ear, "we are both in the decoration business. I hope you recognize your own work, my dear Schinner," he added, pointing to the ceiling of the salon.

"Monseigneur," replied the artist, "I did wrong to take such a celebrated name out of mere bravado; but this day will oblige me to do fine things for you, and so bring credit on my own name of Joseph Bridau."

"You took up my defence," said the count, hastily; "and I hope you will give me the pleasure of dining with me, as well as my lively friend Mistigris."

"Your Excellency doesn't know to what you expose yourself," said the saucy rapin; "'facilis descensus victuali,' as we say at the Black Hen."

"Bridau!" exclaimed the minister, struck by a sudden thought. "Are you any relation to one of the most devoted toilers under the Empire, the head of a bureau, who fell a victim to his zeal?"

"His son, monseigneur," replied Joseph, bowing.

"Then you are most welcome here," said the count, taking Bridau's hand in both of his. "I knew your father, and you can count on me as on—on an uncle in America," added the count, laughing. "But you are too young to have pupils of your own; to whom does Mistigris really belong?"

"To my friend Schinner, who lent him to me," said Joseph. "Mistigris' name is Leon de Lora. Monseigneur, if you knew my father, will you deign to think of his other son, who is now accused of plotting against the State, and is soon to be tried before the Court of Peers?"

"Ah! that's true," said the count. "Yes, I will think about it, be sure of that. As for Colonel Czerni-Georges, the friend of Ali Pacha, and Mina's aide-de-camp—" he continued, walking up to Georges.

"He! why that's my second clerk!" cried Crottat.

"You are quite mistaken, Maitre Crottat," said the count, assuming a stern air. "A clerk who intends to be a notary does not leave important deeds in a diligence at the mercy of other travellers; neither does he spend twenty francs between Paris and Moisselles; or expose himself to be arrested as a deserter—"

"Monseigneur," said Georges Marest, "I may have amused myself with the bourgeois in the diligence, but—"

"Let his Excellency finish what he was saying," said the notary, digging his elbow into his clerk's ribs.

"A notary," continued the count, "ought to practise discretion, shrewdness, caution from the start; he should be incapable of such a blunder as taking a peer of France for a tallow-chandler—"

"I am willing to be blamed for my faults," said Georges; "but I never left my deeds at the mercy of—"

"Now you are committing the fault of contradicting the word of a minister of State, a gentleman, an old man, and a client," said the count. "Give me that deed of sale."

Georges turned over and over the papers in his portfolio.

"That will do; don't disarrange those papers," said the count, taking the deed from his pocket. "Here is what you are looking for."

Crottat turned the paper back and forth, so astonished was he at receiving it from the hands of his client.

"What does this mean, monsieur?" he said, finally, to Georges.

"If I had not taken it," said the count, "Pere Leger,—who is by no means such a ninny as you thought him from his questions about agriculture, by which he showed that he attended to his own business,— Pere Leger might have seized that paper and guessed my purpose. You must give me the pleasure of dining with me, but one on condition,— that of describing, as you promised, the execution of the Muslim of Smyrna, and you must also finish the memoirs of some client which you have certainly read to be so well informed."

"Schlague for blague!" said Leon de Lora, in a whisper, to Joseph Bridau.

"Gentlemen," said the count to the two notaries and Messieurs Margueron and de Reybert, "let us go into the next room and conclude this business before dinner, because, as my friend Mistigris would say: 'Qui esurit constentit.'"

"Well, he is very good-natured," said Leon de Lora to Georges Marest, when the count had left the room.

"Yes, HE may be, but my master isn't," said Georges, "and he will request me to go and bloguer somewhere else."

"Never mind, you like travel," said Bridau.

"What a dressing that boy will get from Monsieur and Madame Moreau!" cried Mistigris.

"Little idiot!" said Georges. "If it hadn't been for him the count would have been amused. Well, anyhow, the lesson is a good one; and if ever again I am caught bragging in a public coach—"

"It is a stupid thing to do," said Joseph Bridau.

"And common," added Mistigris. "'Vulgarity is the brother of pretension.'"

While the matter of the sale was being settled between Monsieur Margueron and the Comte de Serizy, assisted by their respective notaries in presence of Monsieur de Reybert, the ex-steward walked with slow steps to his own house. There he entered the salon and sat down without noticing anything. Little Husson, who was present, slipped into a corner, out of sight, so much did the livid face of his mother's friend alarm him.

"Eh! my friend!" said Estelle, coming into the room, somewhat tired with what she had been doing. "What is the matter?"

"My dear, we are lost,—lost beyond recovery. I am no longer steward of Presles, no longer in the count's confidence."

"Why not?"

"Pere Leger, who was in Pierrotin's coach, told the count all about the affair of Les Moulineaux. But that is not the thing that has cost me his favor."

"What then?"

"Oscar spoke ill of the countess, and he told about the count's diseases."

"Oscar!" cried Madame Moreau. "Ah! my dear, your sin has found you out. It was well worth while to warm that young serpent in your bosom. How often I have told you—"

"Enough!" said Moreau, in a strained voice.

At this moment Estelle and her husband discovered Oscar cowering in his corner. Moreau swooped down on the luckless lad like a hawk on its prey, took him by the collar of the coat and dragged him to the light of a window. "Speak! what did you say to monseigneur in that coach? What demon let loose your tongue, you who keep a doltish silence whenever I speak to you? What did you do it for?" cried the steward, with frightful violence.

Too bewildered to weep, Oscar was dumb and motionless as a statue.

"Come with me and beg his Excellency's pardon," said Moreau.

"As if his Excellency cares for a little toad like that!" cried the furious Estelle.

"Come, I say, to the chateau," repeated Moreau.

Oscar dropped like an inert mass to the ground.

"Come!" cried Moreau, his anger increasing at every instant.

"No! no! mercy!" cried Oscar, who could not bring himself to submit to a torture that seemed to him worse than death.

Moreau then took the lad by his coat, and dragged him, as he might a dead body, through the yards, which rang with the boy's outcries and sobs. He pulled him up the portico, and, with an arm that fury made powerful, he flung him, bellowing, and rigid as a pole, into the salon, at the very feet of the count, who, having completed the purchase of Les Moulineaux, was about to leave the salon for the dining-room with his guests.

"On your knees, wretched boy! and ask pardon of him who gave food to your mind by obtaining your scholarship."

Oscar, his face to the ground, was foaming with rage, and did not say a word. The spectators of the scene were shocked. Moreau seemed no longer in his senses; his face was crimson with injected blood.

"This young man is a mere lump of vanity," said the count, after waiting a moment for Oscar's excuses. "A proud man humiliates himself because he sees there is grandeur in a certain self-abasement. I am afraid that you will never make much of that lad."

So saying, his Excellency passed on. Moreau took Oscar home with him; and on the way gave orders that the horses should immediately be put to Madame Moreau's caleche.

# CHAPTER VII

## A MOTHER'S TRIALS

While the horses were being harnessed, Moreau wrote the following letter to Madame Clapart:—

My dear,—Oscar has ruined me. During his journey in Pierrotin's coach, he spoke of Madame de Serizy's behavior to his Excellency, who was travelling incognito, and actually told, to himself, the secret of his terrible malady. After dismissing me from my stewardship, the count told me not to let Oscar sleep at Presles, but to send him away immediately. Therefore, to obey his orders, the horses are being harnessed at this moment to my wife's carriage, and Brochon, my stable-man, will take the miserable child to you to-night.

We are, my wife and I, in a distress of mind which you may perhaps imagine, though I cannot describe it to you. I will see you in a few days, for I must take another course. I have three children, and I ought to consider their future. At present I do not know what to do; but I shall certainly endeavor to make the count aware of what seventeen years of the life of a man like myself is worth. Owning at the present moment about two hundred and fifty thousand francs, I want to raise myself to a fortune which may some day make me the equal of his Excellency. At this moment I feel within me the power to move mountains and vanquish insurmountable difficulties. What a lever is such a scene of bitter humiliation as I have just passed through! Whose blood has Oscar in his veins? His conduct has been that of a blockhead; up to this moment when I write to you, he has not said a word nor answered, even by a sign, the questions my wife and I have put to him. Will he become an idiot? or is he one already? Dear friend, why did you not instruct him as to his behavior before you sent him to me? How many misfortunes you would have spared me, had you brought him here yourself as I begged you to do. If Estelle alarmed you, you might have stayed at Moisselles. However, the thing is done, and there is no use talking about it.

Adieu; I shall see you soon.

Your devoted servant and friend,
Moreau

At eight o'clock that evening, Madame Clapart, just returned from a walk she had taken with her husband, was knitting winter socks for Oscar, by the light of a single candle. Monsieur Clapart was expecting a friend named Poiret, who often came in to play dominoes, for never did he allow himself to spend an evening at a cafe. In spite of the prudent economy to which his small means forced him, Clapart would not have answered for his temperance amid a luxury of food and in presence of the usual guests of a cafe whose inquisitive observation would have piqued him.

"I'm afraid Poiret came while we were out," said Clapart to his wife.

"Why, no, my friend; the portress would have told us so when we came in," replied Madame Clapart.

"She may have forgotten it."

"What makes you think so?"

"It wouldn't be the first time she has forgotten things for us,—for God knows how people without means are treated."

"Well," said the poor woman, to change the conversation and escape Clapart's cavilling, "Oscar must be at Presles by this time. How he will enjoy that fine house and the beautiful park."

"Oh! yes," snarled Clapart, "you expect fine things of him; but, mark my words, there'll be squabbles wherever he goes."

"Will you never cease to find fault with that poor child?" said the mother. "What has he done to you? If some day we should live at our ease, we may owe it all to him; he has such a good heart—"

"Our bones will be jelly long before that fellow makes his way in the world," cried Clapart. "You don't know your own child; he is conceited, boastful, deceitful, lazy, incapable of—"

"Why don't you go to meet Poiret?" said the poor mother, struck to the heart by the diatribe she had brought upon herself.

"A boy who has never won a prize at school!" continued Clapart.

To bourgeois eyes, the obtaining of school prizes means the certainty of a fine future for the fortunate child.

"Did you win any?" asked his wife. "Oscar stood second in philosophy."

This remark imposed silence for a moment on Clapart; but presently he began again.

"Besides, Madame Moreau hates him like poison, you know why. She'll try to set her husband against him. Oscar to step into his shoes as steward of Presles! Why he'd have to learn agriculture, and know how to survey."

"He can learn."

"He—that pussy cat! I'll bet that if he does get a place down there, it won't be a week before he does some doltish thing which will make the count dismiss him."

"Good God! how can you be so bitter against a poor child who is full of good qualities, sweet-tempered as an angel, incapable of doing harm to any one, no matter who."

Just then the cracking of a postilion's whip and the noise of a carriage stopping before the house was heard, this arrival having apparently put the whole street into a commotion. Clapart, who heard the opening of many windows, looked out himself to see what was happening.

"They have sent Oscar back to you in a post-chaise," he cried, in a tone of satisfaction, though in truth he felt inwardly uneasy.

"Good heavens! what can have happened to him?" cried the poor mother, trembling like a leaf shaken by the autumn wind.

Brochon here came up, followed by Oscar and Poiret.

"What has happened?" repeated the mother, addressing the stable-man.

"I don't know, but Monsieur Moreau is no longer steward of Presles, and they say your son has caused it. His Excellency ordered that he should be sent home to you. Here's a letter from poor Monsieur Moreau, madame, which will tell you all. You never saw a man so changed in a single day."

"Clapart, two glasses of wine for the postilion and for monsieur!" cried the mother, flinging herself into a chair that she might read the fatal letter. "Oscar," she said, staggering towards her bed, "do you want to kill your mother? After all the cautions I gave you this morning—"

She did not end her sentence, for she fainted from distress of mind. When she came to herself she heard her husband saying to Oscar, as he shook him by the arm:—

"Will you answer me?"

"Go to bed, monsieur," she said to her son. "Let him alone, Monsieur Clapart. Don't drive him out of his senses; he is frightfully changed."

Oscar did not hear his mother's last words; he had slipped away to bed the instant that he got the order.

Those who remember their youth will not be surprised to learn that after a day so filled with events and emotions, Oscar, in spite of the enormity of his offences, slept the sleep of the just. The next day he did not find the world so changed as he thought it; he was surprised to be very hungry,—he who the night before had regarded himself as unworthy to live. He had only suffered mentally. At his age mental impressions succeed each other so rapidly that the last weakens its predecessor, however deeply the first may have been cut in. For this reason corporal punishment, though philanthropists are deeply opposed to it in these days, becomes necessary in certain cases for certain children. It is, moreover, the most natural form of retribution, for Nature herself employs it; she uses pain to impress a lasting memory of her precepts. If to the shame of the preceding evening, unhappily too transient, the steward had joined some personal chastisement, perhaps the lesson might have been complete. The discernment with which such punishment needs to be administered is the greatest argument against it. Nature is never mistaken; but the teacher is, and frequently.

Madame Clapart took pains to send her husband out, so that she might be alone with her son the next morning. She was in a state to excite pity. Her eyes, worn with tears; her face, weary with the fatigue of a sleepless night; her feeble voice,—in short, everything about her proved an excess of suffering she could not have borne a second time, and appealed to sympathy.

When Oscar entered the room she signed to him to sit down beside her, and reminded him in a gentle but grieved voice of the benefits they had so constantly received from the steward of Presles. She told him that they had lived, especially for the last six years, on the delicate charity of Monsieur Moreau; and that Monsieur Clapart's salary, also the "demi-bourse," or scholarship, by which he (Oscar) had obtained an education, was due to the Comte de Serizy. Most of this would now cease. Monsieur Clapart, she said, had no claim to a pension,—his period of service not being long enough to obtain one. On the day when he was no longer able to keep his place, what would become of them?

"For myself," she said, "by nursing the sick, or living as a housekeeper in some great family, I could support myself and Monsieur Clapart; but you, Oscar, what could you do? You have no means, and you must earn some, for you must live. There are but four careers for a young man like you,—commerce, government employment, the licensed professions, or military service. All forms of commerce need capital, and we have none to give you. In place of capital, a young man can only give devotion and his capacity. But commerce also demands the utmost discretion, and your conduct yesterday proves that you lack it. To enter a government office, you must go through a long probation by the help of influence, and you have just alienated the only protector that we had,—a most powerful one. Besides, suppose you were to meet with some extraordinary help, by which a young man makes his way promptly either in business or in the public employ, where could you find the money to live and clothe yourself during the time that you are learning your employment?"

Here the mother wandered, like other women, into wordy lamentation: What should she do now to feed the family, deprived of the benefits Moreau's stewardship had enabled him to send her from Presles? Oscar had overthrown his benefactor's prosperity! As commerce and a government clerkship were now impossible, there remained only the professions of notary and lawyer, either barristers or solicitors, and sheriffs. But for those he must study at least three years, and pay considerable sums for entrance fees, examinations, certificates, and diplomas; and here again the question of maintenance presented itself.

"Oscar," she said, in conclusion, "in you I had put all my pride, all my life. In accepting for myself an unhappy old age, I fastened my eyes on you; I saw you with the prospect of a fine career, and I imagined you succeeding in it. That thought, that hope, gave me courage to face the privations I have endured for six years in order to carry you through school, where you have cost me, in spite of the scholarship, between seven and eight hundred francs a year. Now that my hope is vanishing, your future terrifies me. I cannot take one penny from Monsieur Clapart's salary for my son. What can you do? You are not strong enough to mathematics to enter any of the technical schools; and, besides, where could I get the three thousand francs board-money which they extract? This is life as it is, my child. You are eighteen, you are strong. Enlist in the army; it is your only means, that I can see, to earn your bread."

Oscar knew as yet nothing whatever of life. Like all children who have been kept from a knowledge of the trials and poverty of the home, he was ignorant of the necessity of earning his living. The word "commerce" presented no idea whatever to his mind; "public employment" said almost as little, for he saw no results of it. He listened, therefore, with a submissive air, which he tried to make humble, to his mother's exhortations, but they were lost in the void, and did not reach his mind. Nevertheless, the word "army," the thought of being a soldier, and the sight of his mother's tears did at last make him cry. No sooner did Madame Clapart see the drops coursing down his cheeks than she felt herself helpless, and, like most mothers in such cases, she began the peroration which terminates these scenes,—scenes in which they suffer their own anguish and that of their children also.

"Well, Oscar, *promise* me that you will be more discreet in future,—that you will not talk heedlessly any more, but will strive to repress your silly vanity," et cetera, et cetera.

Oscar of course promised all his mother asked him to promise, and then, after gently drawing him to her, Madame Clapart ended by kissing him to console him for being scolded.

"In future," she said, "you will listen to your mother, and will follow her advice; for a mother can give nothing but good counsel to her child. We will go and see your uncle Cardot; that is our last hope. Cardot owed a great deal to your father, who gave him his sister, Mademoiselle Husson, with an enormous dowry for those days, which enabled him to make a large fortune in the silk trade. I think he might, perhaps, place you with Monsieur Camusot, his successor and son-in-law, in the rue des Bourdonnais. But, you see, your uncle Cardot has four children. He gave his establishment, the Cocon d'Or, to his eldest daughter, Madame Camusot; and though Camusot has millions, he has also four children by two wives; and, besides, he scarcely knows of our existence. Cardot has married his second daughter, Mariane, to Monsieur Protez, of the firm of Protez and Chiffreville. The practice of his eldest son, the notary, cost him four hundred thousand francs; and he has just put his second son, Joseph, into the drug business of Matifat. So you see, your uncle Cardot has many reasons not to take an interest in you, whom he sees only four times a year. He has never come to call upon me here, though he was ready enough to visit me at Madame Mere's when he wanted to sell his silks to the Emperor, the imperial highnesses, and all the great people at court. But now the Camusots have turned ultras. The eldest son of Camusot's first wife married a daughter of one of the king's ushers. The world is mighty hump-backed when it stoops! However, it was a clever thing to do, for the Cocon d'Or has the custom of the present court as it had that of the Emperor. But to-morrow we will go and see your uncle Cardot, and I hope that you will endeavor to behave properly; for, as I said before, and I repeat it, that is our last hope."

Monsieur Jean-Jerome-Severin Cardot had been a widower six years. As head-clerk of the Cocon d'Or, one of the oldest firms in Paris, he had bought the establishment in 1793, at a time when the heads of the house were ruined by the maximum; and the money of Mademoiselle Husson's dowry had enabled him to do this, and so make a fortune that was almost colossal in ten years. To establish his children richly during his lifetime, he had conceived the idea of buying an annuity for himself and his wife with three hundred thousand francs, which gave him an income of thirty thousand francs a year. He then divided his capital into three shares of four hundred thousand francs each, which he gave to three of his children,—the Cocon d'Or, given to his eldest daughter on her marriage, being the equivalent of a fourth share. Thus the worthy man, who was now nearly seventy years old, could spend his thirty thousand a year as he pleased, without feeling that he injured the prospects of his children, all finely provided for, whose attentions and proofs of affection were, moreover, not prompted by self-interest.

Uncle Cardot lived at Belleville, in one of the first houses above the Courtille. He there occupied, on the first floor, an apartment overlooking the valley of the Seine, with a southern exposure, and the exclusive enjoyment of a large garden, for the sum of a thousand francs a year. He troubled himself not at all about the three or four other tenants of the same vast country-house. Certain, through a long lease, of ending his days there, he lived rather plainly, served by an old cook and the former maid of the late Madame Cardot,—both of whom expected to reap an annuity of some six hundred francs apiece on the old man's death. These two women took the utmost care of him, and were all the more interested in doing so because no one was ever less fussy or less fault-finding than he. The apartment, furnished by the late Madame Cardot, had remained in the same condition for the last six years,—the old man being perfectly contented with it. He spent in all not more than three thousand francs a year there; for he dined in Paris five days in the week, and returned home at midnight in a hackney-coach, which belonged to an establishment at Courtille. The cook had only her master's breakfast to provide on those days. This was served at eleven o'clock; after that he dressed and perfumed himself, and departed for Paris. Usually, a bourgeois gives notice in the household if he dines out; old Cardot, on the contrary, gave notice when he dined at home.

This little old man—fat, rosy, squat, and strong—always looked, in popular speech, as if he had stepped from a bandbox. He appeared in black silk stockings, breeches of "pou-de-soie" (paduasoy), a white pique waistcoat, dazzling shirt-front, a blue-bottle coat, violet silk gloves, gold buckles to his shoes and his breeches, and, lastly, a touch of powder and a little queue tied with black ribbon. His face was remarkable for a pair of eyebrows as thick as bushes, beneath which sparkled his gray eyes; and for a square nose, thick and long, which gave him somewhat the air of the abbes of former times. His countenance did not belie him. Pere Cardot belonged to that race of lively Gerontes which is now disappearing rapidly, though it once served as Turcarets to the comedies and tales of the eighteenth century. Uncle Cardot always said "Fair lady," and he placed in their carriages, and otherwise paid attention to those women whom he saw without protectors; he "placed himself at their disposition," as he said, in his chivalrous way.

But beneath his calm air and his snowy poll he concealed an old age almost wholly given up to mere pleasure. Among men he openly professed epicureanism, and gave himself the license of free talk. He had seen no harm in the devotion of his son-in-law, Camusot, to Mademoiselle Coralie, for he himself was secretly the Mecaenas of Mademoiselle Florentine, the first danseuse at the Gaiete. But this life and these opinions never appeared in his own home, nor in his external conduct before the world. Uncle Cardot, grave and polite, was thought to be somewhat cold, so much did he affect decorum; a "devote" would have called him a hypocrite.

The worthy old gentleman hated priests; he belonged to that great flock of ninnies who subscribed to the "Constitutionnel," and was much concerned about "refusals to bury." He adored Voltaire, though his preferences were really for Piron, Vade, and Colle. Naturally, he admired Beranger, whom he wittily called the "grandfather of the religion of Lisette." His daughters, Madame Camusot and Madame Protez, and his two sons would, to use a popular expression, have been flabbergasted if any one had explained to them what their father meant by "singing la Mere Godichon."

This long-headed parent had never mentioned his income to his children, who, seeing that he lived in a cheap way, reflected that he had deprived himself of his property for their sakes, and, therefore, redoubled their attentions and tenderness. In fact, he would sometimes say to his sons:—

"Don't lose your property; remember, I have none to leave you."

Camusot, in whom he recognized a certain likeness to his own nature, and whom he liked enough to make a sharer in his secret pleasures, alone knew of the thirty thousand a year annuity. But Camusot approved of the old man's ethics, and thought that, having made the happiness of his children and nobly fulfilled his duty by them, he now had a right to end his life jovially.

"Don't you see, my friend," said the former master of the Cocon d'Or, "I might re-marry. A young woman would give me more children. Well, Florentine doesn't cost me what a wife would; neither does she bore me; and she won't give me children to lessen your property."

Camusot considered that Pere Cardot gave expression to a high sense of family duty in these words; he regarded him as an admirable father-in-law.

"He knows," thought he, "how to unite the interests of his children with the pleasures which old age naturally desires after the worries of business life."

Neither the Cardots, nor the Camusots, nor the Protez knew anything of the ways of life of their aunt Clapart. The family intercourse was restricted to the sending of notes of "faire part" on the occasion of deaths and marriages, and cards at the New Year. The proud Madame Clapart would never have brought herself to seek them were it not for Oscar's interests, and because of her friendship for Moreau, the only person who had been faithful to her in misfortune. She had never annoyed old Cardot by her visits, or her importunities, but she held to him as to a hope, and always went to see him once every three months and talked to him of Oscar, the nephew of the late respectable Madame Cardot; and she took the boy to call upon him three times during each vacation. At each of these visits the old gentleman had given Oscar a dinner at the Cadran-Bleu, taking him, afterwards, to the Gaiete, and returning him safely to the rue de la Cerisaie. On one occasion, having given the boy an entirely new suit of clothes, he added the silver cup and fork and spoon required for his school outfit.

Oscar's mother endeavored to impress the old gentleman with the idea that his nephew cherished him, and she constantly referred to the cup and the fork and spoon and to the beautiful suit of clothes, though nothing was then left of the latter but the waistcoat. But such little arts did Oscar more harm than good when practised on so sly an old fox as uncle Cardot. The latter had never much liked his departed wife, a tall, spare, red-haired woman; he was also aware of the circumstances of the late Husson's marriage with Oscar's mother, and without in the least condemning her, he knew very well that Oscar was a posthumous child. His nephew, therefore, seemed to him to have no claims on the Cardot family. But Madame Clapart, like all women who concentrate their whole being into the sentiment of motherhood, did not put herself in Cardot's place and see the matter from his point of view; she thought he must certainly be interested in so sweet a child, who bore the maiden name of his late wife.

"Monsieur," said old Cardot's maid-servant, coming out to him as he walked about the garden while awaiting his breakfast, after his hairdresser had duly shaved him and powdered his queue, "the mother of your nephew, Oscar, is here."

"Good-day, fair lady," said the old man, bowing to Madame Clapart, and wrapping his white pique dressing-gown about him. "Hey, hey! how this little fellow grows," he added, taking Oscar by the ear.

"He has finished school, and he regretted so much that his dear uncle was not present at the distribution of the Henri IV. prizes, at which he was named. The name of Husson, which, let us hope, he will bear worthily, was proclaimed—"

"The deuce it was!" exclaimed the little old man, stopping short. Madame Clapart, Oscar, and he were walking along a terrace flanked by oranges, myrtles, and pomegranates. "And what did he get?"

"The fourth rank in philosophy," replied the mother proudly.

"Oh! oh!" cried uncle Cardot, "the rascal has a good deal to do to make up for lost time; for the fourth rank in philosophy, well, *it isn't Peru*, you know! You will stay and breakfast with me?" he added.

"We are at your orders," replied Madame Clapart. "Ah! my dear Monsieur Cardot, what happiness it is for fathers and mothers when their children make a good start in life! In this respect—indeed, in all others," she added, catching herself up, "you are one of the most fortunate fathers I have ever known. Under your virtuous son-in-law and your amiable daughter, the Cocon d'Or continues to be the greatest establishment of its kind in Paris. And here's your eldest son, for the last ten years at the head of a fine practice and married to wealth. And you have such charming little granddaughters! You are, as it were, the head of four great families. Leave us, Oscar; go and look at the garden, but don't touch the flowers."

"Why, he's eighteen years old!" said uncle Cardot, smiling at this injunction, which made an infant of Oscar.

"Alas, yes, he is eighteen, my good Monsieur Cardot; and after bringing him so far, sound and healthy in mind and body, neither bow-legged nor crooked, after sacrificing everything to give him an education, it would be hard if I could not see him on the road to fortune."

"That Monsieur Moreau who got him the scholarship will be sure to look after his career," said uncle Cardot, concealing his hypocrisy under an air of friendly good-humor.

"Monsieur Moreau may die," she said. "And besides, he has quarrelled irrevocably with the Comte de Serizy, his patron."

"The deuce he has! Listen, madame; I see you are about to—"

"No, monsieur," said Oscar's mother, interrupting the old man, who, out of courtesy to the "fair lady," repressed his annoyance at being interrupted. "Alas, you do not know the miseries of a mother who, for seven years past, has been forced to take a sum of six hundred francs a year for her son's education from the miserable eighteen hundred francs of her husband's salary. Yes, monsieur, that is all we have had to live upon. Therefore, what more can I do for my poor Oscar? Monsieur Clapart so hates the child that it is impossible for me to keep him in the house. A poor woman, alone in the world, am I not right to come and consult the only relation my Oscar has under heaven?"

"Yes, you are right," said uncle Cardot. "You never told me of all this before."

"Ah, monsieur!" replied Madame Clapart, proudly, "you were the last to whom I would have told my wretchedness. It is all my own fault; I married a man whose incapacity is almost beyond belief. Yes, I am, indeed, most unhappy."

"Listen to me, madame," said the little old man, "and don't weep; it is most painful to me to see a fair lady cry. After all, your son bears the name of Husson, and if my dear deceased wife were living she would wish to do something for the name of her father and of her brother—"

"She loved her brother," said Oscar's mother.

"But all my fortune is given to my children, who expect nothing from me at my death," continued the old man. "I have divided among them the millions that I had, because I wanted to see them happy and enjoying their wealth during my lifetime. I have nothing now except an annuity; and at my age one clings to old habits. Do you know the path on which you ought to start this young fellow?" he went on, after calling to Oscar and taking him by the arm. "Let him study law; I'll pay the costs. Put him in a lawyer's office and let him learn the business of pettifogging; if he does well, if he distinguishes himself, if he likes his profession and I am still alive, each of my children shall, when the proper time comes, lend him a quarter of the cost of a practice; and I will be security for him. You will only have to feed and clothe him. Of course he'll sow a few wild oats, but he'll learn life. Look at me: I left Lyon with two double louis which my grandmother gave me, and walked to Paris; and what am I now? Fasting is good for the health. Discretion, honesty, and work, young man, and you'll succeed. There's a great deal of pleasure in earning one's fortune; and if a man keeps his teeth he eats what he likes in his old age, and sings, as I do, 'La Mere Godichon.' Remember my words: Honesty, work, discretion."

131

"Do you hear that, Oscar?" said his mother. "Your uncle sums up in three words all that I have been saying to you. You ought to carve the last word in letters of fire on your memory."

"Oh, I have," said Oscar.

"Very good,—then thank your uncle; didn't you hear him say he would take charge of your future? You will be a lawyer in Paris."

"He doesn't see the grandeur of his destiny," said the little old man, observing Oscar's apathetic air. "Well, he's just out of school. Listen, I'm no talker," he continued; "but I have this to say: Remember that at your age honesty and uprightness are maintained only by resisting temptations; of which, in a great city like Paris, there are many at every step. Live in your mother's home, in the garret; go straight to the law-school; from there to your lawyer's office; drudge night and day, and study at home. Become, by the time you are twenty-two, a second clerk; by the time you are twenty-four, head-clerk; be steady, and you will win all. If, moreover, you shouldn't like the profession, you might enter the office of my son the notary, and eventually succeed him. Therefore, work, patience, discretion, honesty,—those are your landmarks."

"God grant that you may live thirty years longer to see your fifth child realizing all we expect from him," cried Madame Clapart, seizing uncle Cardot's hand and pressing it with a gesture that recalled her youth.

"Now come to breakfast," replied the kind old man, leading Oscar by the ear.

During the meal uncle Cardot observed his nephew without appearing to do so, and soon saw that the lad knew nothing of life.

"Send him here to me now and then," he said to Madame Clapart, as he bade her good-bye, "and I'll form him for you."

This visit calmed the anxieties of the poor mother, who had not hoped for such brilliant success. For the next fortnight she took Oscar to walk daily, and watched him tyrannically. This brought matters to the end of October. One morning as the poor household was breakfasting on a salad of herring and lettuce, with milk for a dessert, Oscar beheld with terror the formidable ex-steward, who entered the room and surprised this scene of poverty.

"We are now living in Paris—but not as we lived at Presles," said Moreau, wishing to make known to Madame Clapart the change in their relations caused by Oscar's folly. "I shall seldom be here myself; for I have gone into partnership with Pere Leger and Pere Margueron of Beaumont. We are speculating in land, and we have begun by purchasing the estate of Persan. I am the head of the concern, which has a capital of a million; part of which I have borrowed on my own securities. When I find a good thing, Pere Leger and I examine it; my partners have each a quarter and I a half in the profits; but I do nearly all the work, and for that reason I shall be constantly on the road. My wife lives here, in the faubourg du Roule, very plainly. When we see how the business turns out, if we risk only the profits, and if Oscar behaves himself, we may, perhaps, employ him."

"Ah! my friend, the catastrophe caused by my poor boy's heedlessness may prove to be the cause of your making a brilliant fortune; for, really and truly, you were burying your energy and your capacity at Presles."

Madame Clapart then went on to relate her visit to uncle Cardot, in order to show Moreau that neither she nor her son need any longer be a burden on him.

"He is right, that old fellow," said the ex-steward. "We must hold Oscar in that path with an iron hand, and he will end as a barrister or a notary. But he mustn't leave the track; he must go straight through with it. Ha! I know how to help you. The legal business of land-agents is quite important, and I have heard of a lawyer who has just bought what is called a "titre nu"; that means a practice without clients. He is a young man, hard as an iron bar, eager for work, ferociously active. His name is Desroches. I'll offer him our business on condition that he takes Oscar as a pupil; and I'll ask him to let the boy live with him at nine hundred francs a year, of which I will pay three, so that your son will cost you only six hundred francs, without his living, in future. If the boy ever means to become a man it can only be under a discipline like that. He'll come out of that office, notary, solicitor, or barrister, as he may elect."

"Come, Oscar; thank our kind Monsieur Moreau, and don't stand there like a stone post. All young men who commit follies have not the good fortune to meet with friends who still take an interest in their career, even after they have been injured by them."

"The best way to make your peace with me," said Moreau, pressing Oscar's hand, "is to work now with steady application, and to conduct yourself in future properly."

# CHAPTER VIII

## TRICKS AND FARCES OF THE
## EMBRYO LONG ROBE

Ten days later, Oscar was taken by Monsieur Moreau to Maitre Desroches, solicitor, recently established in the rue de Bethisy, in a vast apartment at the end of a narrow court-yard, for which he was paying a relatively low price.

Desroches, a young man twenty-six years of age, born of poor parents, and brought up with extreme severity by a stern father, had himself known the condition in which Oscar now was. Accordingly, he felt an interest in him, but the sort of interest which alone he could take, checked by the apparent harshness that characterized him. The aspect of this gaunt young man, with a muddy skin and hair cropped like a clothes-brush, who was curt of speech and possessed a piercing eye and a gloomy vivaciousness, terrified the unhappy Oscar.

"We work here day and night," said the lawyer, from the depths of his armchair, and behind a table on which were papers, piled up like Alps. "Monsieur Moreau, we won't kill him; but he'll have to go at our pace. Monsieur Godeschal!" he called out.

Though the day was Sunday, the head-clerk appeared, pen in hand.

"Monsieur Godeschal, here's the pupil of whom I spoke to you. Monsieur Moreau takes the liveliest interest in him. He will dine with us and sleep in the small attic next to your chamber. You will allot the exact time it takes to go to the law-school and back, so that he does not lose five minutes on the way. You will see that he learns the Code and is proficient in his classes; that is to say, after he has done his work here, you will give him authors to read. In short, he is to be under your immediate direction, and I shall keep an eye on it. They want to make him what you have made yourself, a capable head-clerk, against the time when he can take such a place himself. Go with Monsieur Godeschal, my young friend; he'll show you your lodging, and you can settle down in it. Did you notice Godeschal?" continued Desroches, speaking to Moreau. "There's a fellow who, like me, has nothing. His sister Mariette, the famous danseuse, is laying up her money to buy him a practice in ten years. My clerks are young blades who have nothing but their ten fingers to rely upon. So we all, my five clerks and I, work as hard as a dozen ordinary fellows. But in ten years I'll have the finest practice in Paris. In my office, business and clients are a passion, and that's beginning to make itself felt. I took Godeschal from Derville, where he was only just made second clerk. He gets a thousand francs a year from me, and food and lodging. But he's worth it; he is indefatigable. I love him, that fellow! He has managed to live, as I did when a clerk, on six hundred francs a year. What I care for above all is honesty, spotless integrity; and when it is practised in such poverty as that, a man's a man. For the slightest fault of that kind a clerk leaves my office."

"The lad is in a good school," thought Moreau.

For two whole years Oscar lived in the rue de Bethisy, a den of pettifogging; for if ever that superannuated expression was applicable to a lawyer's office, it was so in this case. Under this supervision, both petty and able, he was kept to his regular hours and to his work with such rigidity that his life in the midst of Paris was that of a monk.

At five in the morning, in all weathers, Godeschal woke up. He went down with Oscar to the office, where they always found their master up and working. Oscar then did the errands of the office and prepared his lessons for the law-school,—and prepared them elaborately; for Godeschal, and frequently Desroches himself, pointed out to their pupil authors to be looked through and difficulties to overcome. He was not allowed to leave a single section of the Code until he had thoroughly mastered it to the satisfaction of his chief and Godeschal, who put him through preliminary examinations more searching and longer than those of the law-school. On his return from his classes, where he was kept but a short time, he went to his work in the office; occasionally he was sent to the Palais, but always under the thumb of the rigid Godeschal, till dinner. The dinner was that of his master,—one dish of meat, one of vegetables, and a salad. The dessert consisted of a piece of Gruyere cheese. After dinner, Godeschal and Oscar returned to the office and worked till night. Once a month Oscar went to breakfast with his uncle Cardot, and he spent the Sundays with his mother. From time to time Moreau, when he came to the office about his own affairs, would take Oscar to dine in the Palais-Royal, and to some theatre in the evening. Oscar had been so snubbed by Godeschal and by Desroches for his attempts at elegance that he no longer gave a thought to his clothes.

"A good clerk," Godeschal told him, "should have two black coats, one new, one old, a pair of black trousers, black stockings, and shoes. Boots cost too much. You can't have boots till you are called to the bar. A clerk should never spend more than seven hundred francs a year. Good stout shirts of strong linen are what you want. Ha! when a man starts from nothing to reach fortune, he has to keep down to bare necessities. Look at Monsieur Desroches; he did what we are doing, and see where he is now."

Godeschal preached by example. If he professed the strictest principles of honor, discretion, and honesty, he practised them without assumption, as he walked, as he breathed; such action was the natural play of his soul, as walking and breathing were the natural play of his organs. Eighteen months after Oscar's installation into the office, the second clerk was, for the second time, slightly wrong in his accounts, which were comparatively unimportant. Godeschal said to him in presence of all the other clerks:

"My dear Gaudet, go away from here of your own free will, that it may not be said that Monsieur Desroches has dismissed you. You have been careless or absent-minded, and neither of those defects can pass here. The master shall know nothing about the matter; that is all that I can do for a comrade."

At twenty years of age, Oscar became third clerk in the office. Though he earned no salary, he was lodged and fed, for he did the work of the second clerk. Desroches employed two chief clerks, and the work of the second was unremitting toil. By the end of his second year in the law-school Oscar knew more than most licensed graduates; he did the work at the Palais intelligently, and argued some cases in chambers. Godeschal and Desroches were satisfied with him. And yet, though he now seemed a sensible man, he showed, from time to time, a hankering after pleasure and a desire to shine, repressed, though it was, by the stern discipline and continual toil of his life.

Moreau, satisfied with Oscar's progress, relaxed, in some degree, his watchfulness; and when, in July, 1825, Oscar passed his examinations with a spotless record, the land-agent gave him the money to dress himself elegantly. Madame Clapart, proud and happy in her son, prepared the outfit splendidly for the rising lawyer.

In the month of November, when the courts reopened, Oscar Husson occupied the chamber of the second clerk, whose work he now did wholly. He had a salary of eight hundred francs with board and lodging. Consequently, uncle Cardot, who went privately to Desroches and made inquiries about his nephew, promised Madame Clapart to be on the lookout for a practice for Oscar, if he continued to do as well in the future.

In spite of these virtuous appearances, Oscar Husson was undergoing a great strife in his inmost being. At times he thought of quitting a life so directly against his tastes and his nature. He felt that galley-slaves were happier than he. Galled by the collar of this iron system, wild desires seized him to fly when he compared himself in the street with the well-dressed young men whom he met. Sometimes he was driven by a sort of madness towards women; then, again, he resigned himself, but only to fall into a deeper disgust for life. Impelled by the example of Godeschal, he was forced, rather than led of himself, to remain in that rugged way.

Godeschal, who watched and took note of Oscar, made it a matter of principle not to allow his pupil to be exposed to temptation. Generally the young clerk was without money, or had so little that he could not, if he would, give way to excess. During the last year, the worthy Godeschal had made five or six parties of pleasure with Oscar, defraying the expenses, for he felt that the rope by which he tethered the young kid must be slackened. These "pranks," as he called them, helped Oscar to endure existence, for there was little amusement in breakfasting with his uncle Cardot, and still less in going to see his mother, who lived even more penuriously than Desroches. Moreau could not make himself familiar with Oscar as Godeschal could; and perhaps that sincere friend to young Husson was behind Godeschal in these efforts to initiate the poor youth safely into the mysteries of life. Oscar, grown prudent, had come, through contact with others, to see the extent and the character of the fault he had committed on that luckless journey; but the volume of his repressed fancies and the follies of youth might still get the better of him. Nevertheless, the more knowledge he could get of the world and its laws, the better his mind would form itself, and, provided Godeschal never lost sight of him, Moreau flattered himself that between them they could bring the son of Madame Clapart through in safety.

"How is he getting on?" asked the land-agent of Godeschal on his return from one of his journeys which had kept him some months out of Paris.

"Always too much vanity," replied Godeschal. "You give him fine clothes and fine linen, he wears the shirt-fronts of a stockbroker, and so my dainty coxcomb spends his Sundays in the Tuileries, looking out for adventures. What else can you expect? That's youth. He torments me to present him to my sister, where he would see a pretty sort of society!—actresses, ballet-dancers, elegant young fops, spendthrifts who are wasting their fortunes! His mind, I'm afraid, is not fitted for law. He can talk well, though; and if we could make him a barrister he might plead cases that were carefully prepared for him."

In the month of November, 1825, soon after Oscar Husson had taken possession of his new clerkship, and at the moment when he was about to pass his examination for the licentiate's degree, a new clerk arrived to take the place made vacant by Oscar's promotion.

This fourth clerk, named Frederic Marest, intended to enter the magistracy, and was now in his third year at the law school. He was a fine young man of twenty-three, enriched to the amount of some twelve thousand francs a year by the death of a bachelor uncle, and the son of Madame Marest, widow of the wealthy wood-merchant. This future magistrate, actuated by a laudable desire to understand his vocation in its smallest details, had put himself in Desroches' office for the purpose of studying legal procedure, and of training himself to take a place as head-clerk in two years. He hoped to do his "stage" (the period between the admission as licentiate and the call to the bar) in Paris, in order to be fully prepared for the functions of a post which would surely not be refused to a rich young man. To see himself, by the time he was thirty, "procureur du roi" in any court, no matter where, was his sole ambition. Though Frederic Marest was cousin-german to Georges Marest, the latter not having told his surname in Pierrotin's coucou, Oscar Husson did not connect the present Marest with the grandson of Czerni-Georges.

"Messieurs," said Godeschal at breakfast time, addressing all the clerks, "I announce to you the arrival of a new jurisconsult; and as he is rich, rishissime, we will make him, I hope, pay a glorious entrance-fee."

"Forward, the book!" cried Oscar, nodding to the youngest clerk, "and pray let us be serious."

The youngest clerk climbed like a squirrel along the shelves which lined the room, until he could reach a register placed on the top shelf, where a thick layer of dust had settled on it.

"It is getting colored," said the little clerk, exhibiting the volume.

We must explain the perennial joke of this book, then much in vogue in legal offices. In a clerical life where work is the rule, amusement is all the more treasured because it is rare; but, above all, a hoax or a practical joke is enjoyed with delight. This fancy or custom does, to a certain extent, explain Georges Marest's behavior in the coucou. The gravest and most gloomy clerk is possessed, at times, with a craving for fun and quizzing. The instinct with which a set of young clerks will seize and develop a hoax or a practical joke is really marvellous. The denizens of a studio and of a lawyer's office are, in this line, superior to comedians.

In buying a practice without clients, Desroches began, as it were, a new dynasty. This circumstance made a break in the usages relative to the reception of new-comers. Moreover, Desroches having taken an office where legal documents had never yet been scribbled, had bought new tables, and white boxes edged with blue, also new. His staff was made up of clerks coming from other officers, without mutual ties, and surprised, as one may say, to find themselves together. Godeschal, who had served his apprenticeship under Maitre Derville, was not the sort of clerk to allow the precious tradition of the "welcome" to be lost. This "welcome" is a breakfast which every neophyte must give to the "ancients" of the office into which he enters.

Now, about the time when Oscar came to the office, during the first six months of Desroches' installation, on a winter evening when the work had been got through more quickly than usual, and the clerks were warming themselves before the fire preparatory to departure, it came into Godeschal's head to construct and compose a Register "architriclino-basochien," of the utmost antiquity, saved from the fires of the Revolution, and derived through the procureur of the Chatelet-Bordin, the immediate predecessor of Sauvaguest, the attorney, from whom Desroches had bought his practice. The work, which was highly approved by the other clerks, was begun by a search through all the dealers in old paper for a register, made of paper with the mark of the eighteenth century, duly bound in parchment, on which should be the stamp of an order in council. Having found such a volume it was left about in the dust, on the stove, on the ground, in the kitchen, and even in what the clerks called the "chamber of deliberations"; and thus it obtained a mouldiness to delight an antiquary, cracks of aged dilapidation, and broken corners that looked as though the rats had gnawed them; also, the gilt edges were tarnished with surprising perfection. As soon as the book was duly prepared, the entries were made. The following extracts will show to the most obtuse mind the purpose to which the office of Maitre Desroches devoted this register, the first sixty pages of which were filled with reports of fictitious cases. On the first page appeared as follows, in the legal spelling of the eighteenth century:—

In the name of the Father, Son, and Holy Ghost, so be it. This day, the feast of our lady Saincte-Geneviesve, patron saint of Paris, under whose protection have existed, since the year 1525 the clerks of this Practice, we the under-signed, clerks and sub-clerks of Maistre Jerosme-Sebastien Bordin, successor to the late Guerbet, in his lifetime procureur at the Chastelet, do hereby recognize the obligation under which we lie to renew and continue the register and the archives of installation of the clerks of this noble Practice, a glorious member of the Kingdom of Basoche, the which register, being now full in consequence of the many acts and deeds of our well-beloved predecessors, we have consigned to the Keeper of the Archives of the Palais for safe-keeping, with the registers of other ancient Practices; and we have ourselves gone, each and all, to hear mass at the parish church of Saint-Severin to solemnize the inauguration of this our new register.

In witness whereof we have hereunto signed our names: Malin, head-clerk; Grevin, second-clerk; Athanase Feret, clerk; Jacques

Heret, clerk; Regnault de Saint-Jean-d'Angely, clerk; Bedeau, youngest clerk and gutter-jumper.

In the year of our Lord 1787.

After the mass aforesaid was heard, we conveyed ourselves to Courtille, where, at the common charge, we ordered a fine breakfast; which did not end till seven o'clock the next morning.

This was marvellously well engrossed. An expert would have said that it was written in the eighteenth century. Twenty-seven reports of receptions of neophytes followed, the last in the fatal year of 1792. Then came a blank of fourteen years; after which the register began again, in 1806, with the appointment of Bordin as attorney before the first Court of the Seine. And here follows the deed which proclaimed the reconstitution of the kingdom of Basoche:—

God in his mercy willed that, in spite of the fearful storms which have cruelly ravaged the land of France, now become a great Empire, the archives of the very celebrated Practice of Maitre Bordin should be preserved; and we, the undersigned, clerks of the very virtuous and very worthy Maitre Bordin, do not hesitate to attribute this unheard-of preservation, when all titles, privileges, and charters were lost, to the protection of Sainte-Genevieve, patron Saint of this office, and also to the reverence which the last of the procureurs of noble race had for all that belonged to ancient usages and customs. In the uncertainty of knowing the exact part of Sainte-Genevieve and Maitre Bordin in this miracle, we have resolved, each of us, to go to Saint-Etienne du Mont and there hear mass, which will be said before the altar of that Holy-Shepherdess who sends us sheep to shear, and also to offer a breakfast to our master Bordin, hoping that he will pay the costs.

Signed: Oignard, first clerk; Poidevin, second clerk; Proust, clerk; Augustin Coret, sub-clerk.

At the office.

November, 1806.

At three in the afternoon, the above-named clerks hereby return their grateful thanks to their excellent master, who regaled them at the establishment of the Sieur Rolland restaurateur, rue du Hasard, with exquisite wines of three regions, to wit: Bordeaux, Champagne, and Burgundy, also with dishes most carefully chosen, between the hours of four in the afternoon to half-past seven in the evening. Coffee, ices, and liqueurs were in abundance. But the presence of the master himself forbade the chanting of hymns of praise in clerical stanzas. No clerk exceeded the bounds of amiable gayety, for the worthy, respectable, and generous patron had promised to take his clerks to see Talma in "Brittanicus," at the Theatre-Francais. Long life to Maitre Bordin! May God shed favors on his venerable pow! May he sell dear so glorious a practice! May the rich clients for whom he prays arrive! May his bills of costs and charges be paid in a trice! May our masters to come be like him! May he ever be loved by clerks in other worlds than this!

Here followed thirty-three reports of various receptions of new clerks, distinguished from one another by different writing and different inks, also by quotations, signatures, and praises of good cheer and wines, which seemed to show that each report was written and signed on the spot, "inter pocula."

Finally, under date of the month of June, 1822, the period when Desroches took the oath, appears this constitutional declaration:—

I, the undersigned, Francois-Claude-Marie Godeschal, called by Maitre Desroches to perform the difficult functions of head-clerk in a Practice where the clients have to be created, having learned through Maitre Derville, from whose office I come, of the existence of the famous archives architriclino-basochien, so celebrated at the Palais, have implored our gracious master to obtain them from his predecessor; for it has become of the highest importance to recover a document bearing date of the year 1786, which is connected with other documents deposited for safe-keeping at the Palais, the existence of which has been certified to by Messrs. Terrasse and Duclos, keepers of records, by the help of which we may go back to the year 1525, and find historical indications of the utmost value on the manners, customs, and cookery of the clerical race.

Having received a favorable answer to this request, the present office has this day been put in possession of these proofs of the worship in which our predecessors held the Goddess Bottle and good living.

In consequence thereof, for the edification of our successors, and to renew the chain of years and goblets, I, the said Godeschal, have invited Messieurs Doublet, second clerk; Vassal, third clerk; Herisson and Grandemain, clerks; and Dumets, sub-clerk, to breakfast, Sunday next, at the "Cheval Rouge," on the Quai Saint-Bernard, where we will celebrate the victory of obtaining this volume which contains the Charter of our gullets.

This day, Sunday, June 27th, were imbibed twelve bottles of twelve different wines, regarded as exquisite; also were devoured melons, "pates au jus romanum," and a fillet of beef with mushroom sauce. Mademoiselle Mariette, the illustrious sister of our head-clerk and leading lady of the Royal Academy of music and dancing, having obligingly put at the disposition of this Practice orchestra seats for the performance of this evening, it is proper to make this record of her generosity. Moreover, it is hereby decreed that the aforesaid clerks shall convey themselves in a body to that noble demoiselle to thank her in person, and declare to her that on the occasion of her first lawsuit, if the devil sends her one, she shall pay the money laid out upon it, and no more.

And our head-clerk Godeschal has been and is hereby proclaimed a flower of Basoche, and, more especially, a good fellow. May a man who treats so well be soon in treaty for a Practice of his own!

On this record were stains of wine, pates, and candle-grease. To exhibit the stamp of truth that the writers had managed to put upon these records, we may here give the report of Oscar's own pretended reception:—

This day, Monday, November 25th, 1822, after a session held yesterday at the rue de la Cerisaie, Arsenal quarter, at the house of Madame Clapart, mother of the candidate-basochien Oscar Husson, we, the undersigned, declare that the repast of admission surpassed our expectations. It was composed of radishes, pink and black, gherkins, anchovies, butter and olives for hors-d'oeuvre; a succulent soup of rice, bearing testimony to maternal solicitude, for we recognized therein a delicious taste of poultry; indeed, by acknowledgment of the new member, we learned that the gibbets of a fine stew prepared by the hands of Madame Clapart herself had been judiciously inserted into the family soup-pot with a care that is never taken except in such households.

Item: the said gibbets inclosed in a sea of jelly.

Item: a tongue of beef with tomatoes, which rendered us all tongue-tied automatoes.

Item: a compote of pigeons with caused us to think the angels had had a finger in it.

Item: a timbale of macaroni surrounded by chocolate custards.

Item: a dessert composed of eleven delicate dishes, among which we remarked (in spite of the tipsiness caused by sixteen bottles of the choicest wines) a compote of peaches of august and mirobolant delicacy.

The wines of Roussillon and those of the banks of the Rhone completely effaced those of Champagne and Burgundy. A bottle of maraschino and another of kirsch did, in spite of the exquisite coffee, plunge us into so marked an oenological ecstasy that we found ourselves at a late hour in the Bois de Boulogne instead of our domicile, where we thought we were.

In the statutes of our Order there is one rule which is rigidly enforced; namely, to allow all candidates for the privilege of Basoche to limit the magnificence of their feast of welcome to the length of their purse; for it is publicly notorious that no one delivers himself up to Themis if he has a fortune, and every clerk is, alas, sternly curtailed by his parents. Consequently, we hereby record with the highest praise the liberal conduct of Madame Clapart, widow, by her first marriage, of Monsieur Husson, father of the candidate, who is worthy of the hurrahs which we gave for her at dessert.

To all of which we hereby set our hands.

[Signed by all the clerks.]


Three clerks had already been deceived by the Book, and three real "receptions of welcome," were recorded on this imposing register.

The day after the arrival of each neophyte, the little sub-clerk (the errand-boy and "gutter-jumper") laid upon the new-comer's desk the "Archives Architriclino-Basochiennes," and the clerks enjoyed the sight of his countenance as he studied its facetious pages. Inter pocula each candidate had learned the secret of the farce, and the revelation inspired him with the desire to hoax his successor.

We see now why Oscar, become in his turn participator in the hoax, called out to the little clerk, "Forward, the book!"

Ten minutes later a handsome young man, with a fine figure and pleasant face, presented himself, asked for Monsieur Desroches, and gave his name without hesitation to Godeschal.

"I am Frederic Marest," he said, "and I come to take the place of third clerk."

"Monsieur Husson," said Godeschal to Oscar, "show monsieur his seat and tell him about the customs of the office."

The next day the new clerk found the register lying on his desk. He took it up, but after reading a few pages he began to laugh, said nothing to the assembled clerks, and laid the book down again.

"Messieurs," he said, when the hour of departure came at five o'clock, "I have a cousin who is head clerk of the notary Maitre Leopold Hannequin; I will ask his advice as to what I ought to do for my welcome."

"That looks ill," cried Godeschal, when Frederic had gone, "he hasn't the cut of a novice, that fellow!"

"We'll get some fun out of him yet," said Oscar.

# CHAPTER IX

## LA MARQUISE DE LAS FLORENTINAS Y CABIROLOS

The following day, at two o'clock, a young man entered the office, whom Oscar recognized as Georges Marest, now head-clerk of the notary Hannequin.

"Ha! here's the friend of Ali pacha!" he exclaimed in a flippant way.

"Hey! you here, Monsieur l'ambassadeur!" returned Georges, recollecting Oscar.

"So you know each other?" said Godeschal, addressing Georges.

"I should think so! We got into a scrape together," replied Georges, "about two years ago. Yes, I had to leave Crottat and go to Hannequin in consequence of that affair."

"What was it?" asked Godeschal.

"Oh, nothing!" replied Georges, at a sign from Oscar. "We tried to hoax a peer of France, and he bowled us over. Ah ca! so you want to jockey my cousin, do you?"

"We jockey no one," replied Oscar, with dignity; "there's our charter."

And he presented the famous register, pointing to a place where sentence of banishment was passed on a refractory who was stated to have been forced, for acts of dishonesty, to leave the office in 1788.

Georges laughed as he looked through the archives.

"Well, well," he said, "my cousin and I are rich, and we'll give you a fete such as you never had before,—something to stimulate your imaginations for that register. To-morrow (Sunday) you are bidden to the Rocher de Cancale at two o'clock. Afterwards, I'll take you to spend the evening with Madame la Marquise de las Florentinas y Cabirolos, where we shall play cards, and you'll see the elite of the women of fashion. Therefore, gentleman of the lower courts," he added, with notarial assumption, "you will have to behave yourselves, and carry your wine like the seigneurs of the Regency."

"Hurrah!" cried the office like one man. "Bravo! very well! vivat! Long live the Marests!"

"What's all this about?" asked Desroches, coming out from his private office. "Ah! is that you, Georges? I know what you are after; you want to demoralize my clerks."

So saying, he withdrew into his own room, calling Oscar after him.

"Here," he said, opening his cash-box, "are five hundred francs. Go to the Palais, and get from the registrar a copy of the decision in Vandernesse against Vandernesse; it must be served to-night if possible. I have promised a PROD of twenty francs to Simon. Wait for the copy if it is not ready. Above all, don't let yourself be fooled; for Derville is capable, in the interest of his clients, to stick a spoke in our wheel. Count Felix de Vandernesse is more powerful than his brother, our client, the ambassador. Therefore keep your eyes open, and if there's the slightest hitch come back to me at once."

Oscar departed with the full intention of distinguishing himself in this little skirmish,—the first affair entrusted to him since his installation as second clerk.

After the departure of Georges and Oscar, Godeschal sounded the new clerk to discover the joke which, as he thought, lay behind this Marquise de las Florentinas y Cabirolos. But Frederic, with the coolness and gravity of a king's attorney, continued his cousin's hoax, and by his way of answering, and his manner generally, he succeeded in making the

150

office believe that the marquise might really be the widow of a Spanish grandee, to whom his cousin Georges was paying his addresses. Born in Mexico, and the daughter of Creole parents, this young and wealthy widow was noted for the easy manners and habits of the women of those climates.

"She loves to laugh, she loves to sing, she loves to drink like me!" he said in a low voice, quoting the well-known song of Beranger. "Georges," he added, "is very rich; he has inherited from his father (who was a widower) eighteen thousand francs a year, and with the twelve thousand which an uncle has just left to each of us, he has an income of thirty thousand. So he pays his debts, and gives up the law. He hopes to be Marquis de las Florentinas, for the young widow is marquise in her own right, and has the privilege of giving her titles to her husband."

Though the clerks were still a good deal undecided in mind as to the marquise, the double perspective of a breakfast at the Rocher de Cancale and a fashionable festivity put them into a state of joyous expectation. They reserved all points as to the Spanish lady, intending to judge her without appeal after the meeting.

The Marquise de las Florentinas y Cabirolos was neither more nor less than Mademoiselle Agathe-Florentine Cabirolle, first danseuse at the Gaiete, with whom uncle Cardot was in the habit of singing "Mere Godichon." A year after the very reparable loss of Madame Cardot, the successful merchant encountered Florentine as she was leaving Coulon's dancing-class. Attracted by the beauty of that choregraphic flower (Florentine was then about thirteen years of age), he followed her to the rue Pastourel, where he found that the future star of the ballet was the daughter of a portress. Two weeks later, the mother and daughter, established in the rue de Crussol, were enjoying a modest competence. It was to this protector of the arts—to use the consecrated phrase—that the theatre owed the brilliant danseuse. The generous Maecenas made two beings almost beside themselves with joy in the possession of mahogany furniture, hangings, carpets, and a regular kitchen; he allowed them a woman-of-all-work, and gave them two hundred and fifty francs a month for their living. Pere Cardot, with his hair in "pigeon-wings," seemed like an angel, and was treated with the attention due to a benefactor. To him this was the age of gold.

For three years the warbler of "Mere Godichon" had the wise policy to keep Mademoiselle Cabirolle and her mother in this little apartment, which was only ten steps from the theatre; but he gave the girl, out of love for the choregraphic art, the great Vestris for a master. In 1820 he had the pleasure of seeing Florentine dance her first "pas" in the ballet of a melodrama entitled "The Ruins of Babylon." Florentine was then about sixteen. Shortly after this debut Pere Cardot became an "old screw" in the eyes of his protegee; but as he had the sense to see that a danseuse at the Gaiete had a certain rank to maintain, he raised the monthly stipend to five hundred francs, for which, although he did not again become an angel, he was, at least, a "friend for life," a second father. This was his silver age.

From 1820 to 1823, Florentine had the experience of every danseuse of nineteen to twenty years of age. Her friends were the illustrious Mariette and Tullia, leading ladies of the Opera, Florine, and also poor Coralie, torn too early from the arts, and love, and Camusot. As old Cardot had by this time acquired five additional years, he had fallen into the indulgence of a semi-paternity, which is the way with old men towards the young talents they have trained, and which owe their success to them. Besides, where could he have found another Florentine who knew all his habits and likings, and with whom he and his friends could sing "Mere Godichon"? So the little old man remained under a yoke that was semi-conjugal and also irresistibly strong. This was the brass age for the old fellow.

During the five years of silver and gold Pere Cardot had laid by eighty thousand francs. The old gentleman, wise from experience, foresaw that by the time he was seventy Florentine would be of age, probably engaged at the Opera, and, consequently, wanting all the luxury of a theatrical star.

Some days before the party mentioned by Georges, Pere Cardot had spent the sum of forty-five thousand francs in fitting up for his Florentine the former apartment of the late Coralie. In Paris there are suites of rooms as well as houses and streets that have their predestinations. Enriched with a magnificent service of plate, the "prima danseuse" of the Gaiete began to give dinners, spent three hundred francs a month on her dress, never went out except in a hired carriage, and had a maid for herself, a cook, and a little footman.

In fact, an engagement at the Opera was already in the wind. The Cocon d'Or did homage to its first master by sending its most splendid products for the gratification of Mademoiselle Cabirolle, now called Florentine. The magnificence which suddenly burst upon her apartment in the rue de Vendome would have satisfied the most ambitious supernumerary. After being the master of the ship for seven years, Cardot now found himself towed along by a force of unlimited caprice. But the luckless old gentleman was fond of his tyrant. Florentine was to close his eyes; he meant to leave her a hundred thousand francs. The iron age had now begun.

Georges Marest, with thirty thousand francs a year, and a handsome face, courted Florentine. Every danseuse makes a point of having some young man who will take her to drive, and arrange the gay excursions into the country which all such women delight in. However disinterested she may be, the courtship of such a star is a passion which costs some trifles to the favored mortal. There are dinners at restaurants, boxes at the theatres, carriages to go to the environs and return, choice wines consumed in profusion,—for an opera danseuse eats and drinks like an athlete. Georges amused himself like other young men who pass at a jump from paternal discipline to a rich independence, and the death of his uncle, nearly doubling his means, had still further enlarged his ideas. As long as he had only his patrimony of eighteen thousand francs a year, his intention was to become a notary, but (as his cousin remarked to the clerks of Desroches) a man must be stupid who begins a profession with the fortune most men hope to acquire in order to leave it. Wiser then Georges, Frederic persisted in following the career of public office, and of putting himself, as we have seen, in training for it.

A young man as handsome and attractive as Georges might very well aspire to the hand of a rich creole; and the clerks in Desroches' office, all of them the sons of poor parents, having never frequented the great world, or, indeed, known anything about it, put themselves into their best clothes on the following day, impatient enough to behold, and be presented to the Mexican Marquise de las Florentinas y Cabirolos.

"What luck," said Oscar to Godeschal, as they were getting up in the morning, "that I had just ordered a new coat and trousers and waistcoat, and that my dear mother had made me that fine outfit! I have six frilled shirts of fine linen in the dozen she made for me. We shall make an appearance! Ha! ha! suppose one of us were to carry off the Creole marchioness from that Georges Marest!"

"Fine occupation that, for a clerk in our office!" cried Godeschal. "Will you never control your vanity, popinjay?"

"Ah! monsieur," said Madame Clapart, who entered the room at that moment to bring her son some cravats, and overhead the last words of the head-clerk, "would to God that my Oscar might always follow your advice. It is what I tell him all the time: 'Imitate Monsieur Godeschal; listen to what he tells you.'"

"He'll go all right, madame," interposed Godeschal, "but he mustn't commit any more blunders like one he was guilty of last night, or he'll lose the confidence of the master. Monsieur Desroches won't stand any one not succeeding in what he tells them to do. He ordered your son, for a first employment in his new clerkship, to get a copy of a judgment which ought to have been served last evening, and Oscar, instead of doing so, allowed himself to be fooled. The master was furious. It's a chance if I have been able to repair the mischief by going this morning, at six o'clock, to see the head-clerk at the Palais, who has promised me to have a copy ready by seven o'clock to-morrow morning."

"Ah, Godeschal!" cried Oscar, going up to him and pressing his hand. "You are, indeed, a true friend."

"Ah, monsieur!" said Madame Clapart, "a mother is happy, indeed, in knowing that her son has a friend like you; you may rely upon a gratitude which can end only with my life. Oscar, one thing I want to say to you now. Distrust that Georges Marest. I wish you had never met him again, for he was the cause of your first great misfortune in life."

"Was he? How so?" asked Godeschal.

The too devoted mother explained succinctly the adventure of her poor Oscar in Pierrotin's coucou.

"I am certain," said Godeschal, "that that blagueur is preparing some trick against us for this evening. As for me, I can't go to the Marquise de las Florentinas' party, for my sister wants me to draw up the terms of her new engagement; I shall have to leave after the dessert. But, Oscar, be on your guard. They will ask you to play, and, of course, the Desroches office mustn't draw back; but be careful. You shall play for both of us; here's a hundred francs," said the good fellow, knowing that Oscar's purse was dry from the demands of his tailor and bootmaker. "Be prudent; remember not to play beyond that sum; and don't let yourself get tipsy, either with play or libations. Saperlotte! a second clerk is already a man of weight, and shouldn't gamble on notes, or go beyond a certain limit in anything. His business is to get himself admitted to the bar. Therefore don't drink too much, don't play too long, and maintain a proper dignity,—that's your rule of conduct. Above all, get home by midnight; for, remember, you must be at the Palais to-morrow morning by seven to get that judgment. A man is not forbidden to amuse himself, but business first, my boy."

"Do you hear that, Oscar?" said Madame Clapart. "Monsieur Godeschal is indulgent; see how well he knows how to combine the pleasures of youth and the duties of his calling."

Madame Clapart, on the arrival of the tailor and the bootmaker with Oscar's new clothes, remained alone with Godeschal, in order to return him the hundred francs he had just given her son.

"Ah, monsieur!" she said, "the blessings of a mother will follow you wherever you go, and in all your enterprises."

Poor woman! she now had the supreme delight of seeing her son well-dressed, and she gave him a gold watch, the price of which she had saved by economy, as the reward of his good conduct.

"You draw for the conscription next week," she said, "and to prepare, in case you get a bad number, I have been to see your uncle Cardot. He is very much pleased with you; and so delighted to know you are a second clerk at twenty, and to hear of your successful examination at the law-school, that he promised me the money for a substitute. Are not you glad to think that your own good conduct has brought such reward? Though you have some privations to bear, remember the happiness of being able, five years from now, to buy a practice. And think, too, my dear little kitten, how happy you make your mother."

Oscar's face, somewhat thinned by study, had acquired, through habits of business, a serious expression. He had reached his full growth, his beard was thriving; adolescence had given place to virility. The mother could not refrain from admiring her son and kissing him, as she said:—

"Amuse yourself, my dear boy, but remember the advice of our good Monsieur Godeschal. Ah! by the bye, I was nearly forgetting! Here's a present our friend Moreau sends you. See! what a pretty pocket-book."

"And I want it, too; for the master gave me five hundred francs to get that cursed judgment of Vandernesse versus Vandernesse, and I don't want to leave that sum of money in my room."

"But, surely, you are not going to carry it with you!" exclaimed his mother, in alarm. "Suppose you should lose a sum like that! Hadn't you better give it to Monsieur Godeschal for safe keeping?"

"Godeschal!" cried Oscar, who thought his mother's suggestion excellent.

But Godeschal, who, like all clerks, has his time to himself on Sundays, from ten to two o'clock, had already departed.

When his mother left him, Oscar went to lounge upon the boulevards until it was time to go to Georges Marest's breakfast. Why not display those beautiful clothes which he wore with a pride and joy which all young fellows who have been pinched for means in their youth will remember. A pretty waistcoat with a blue ground and a palm-leaf pattern, a pair of black cashmere trousers pleated, a black coat very well fitting, and a cane with a gilt top, the cost of which he had saved himself, caused a natural joy to the poor lad, who thought of his manner of dress on the day of that journey to Presles, as the effect that Georges had then produced upon him came back to his mind.

Oscar had before him the perspective of a day of happiness; he was to see the gay world at last! Let us admit that a clerk deprived of enjoyments, though longing for dissipation, was likely to let his unchained senses drive the wise counsels of his mother and Godeschal completely out of his mind. To the shame of youth let it be added that good advice is never lacking to it. In the matter of Georges, Oscar himself had a feeling of aversion for him; he felt humiliated before a witness of that scene in the salon at Presles when Moreau had flung him at the count's feet. The moral senses have their laws, which are implacable, and we are always punished for disregarding them. There is one in particular, which the animals themselves obey without discussion, and invariably; it is that which tells us to avoid those who have once injured us, with or without intention, voluntarily or involuntarily. The creature from whom we receive either damage or annoyance will always be displeasing to us. Whatever may be his rank or the degree of affection in which he stands to us, it is best to break away from him; for our evil genius has sent him to us. Though the Christian sentiment is opposed to it, obedience to this terrible law is essentially social and conservative. The daughter of James II., who seated herself upon her father's throne, must have caused him many a wound before that usurpation. Judas had certainly given some murderous blow to Jesus before he betrayed him. We have within us an inward power of sight, an eye of the soul which foresees catastrophes;

and the repugnance that comes over us against the fateful being is the result of that foresight. Though religion orders us to conquer it, distrust remains, and its voice is forever heard. Would Oscar, at twenty years of age, have the wisdom to listen to it?

Alas! when, at half-past two o'clock, Oscar entered the salon of the Rocher de Cancale,—where were three invited persons besides the clerks, to wit: an old captain of dragoons, named Giroudeau; Finot, a journalist who might procure an engagement for Florentine at the Opera, and du Bruel, an author, the friend of Tullia, one of Mariette's rivals,—the second clerk felt his secret hostility vanish at the first handshaking, the first dashes of conversation as they sat around a table luxuriously served. Georges, moreover, made himself charming to Oscar.

"You've taken to private diplomacy," he said; "for what difference is there between a lawyer and an ambassador? only that between a nation and an individual. Ambassadors are the attorneys of Peoples. If I can ever be useful to you, let me know."

"Well," said Oscar, "I'll admit to you now that you once did me a very great harm."

"Pooh!" said Georges, after listening to the explanation for which he asked; "it was Monsieur de Serizy who behaved badly. His wife! I wouldn't have her at any price; neither would I like to be in the count's red skin, minister of State and peer of France as he is. He has a small mind, and I don't care a fig for him now."

Oscar listened with true pleasure to these slurs on the count, for they diminished, in a way, the importance of his fault; and he echoed the spiteful language of the ex-notary, who amused himself by predicting the blows to the nobility of which the bourgeoisie were already dreaming,— blows which were destined to become a reality in 1830.

At half-past three the solid eating of the feast began; the dessert did not appear till eight o'clock,—each course having taken two hours to serve. None but clerks can eat like that! The stomachs of eighteen and twenty are inexplicable to the medical art. The wines were worthy of

Borrel, who in those days had superseded the illustrious Balaine, the creator of the first restaurant for delicate and perfectly prepared food in Paris,—that is to say, the whole world.

The report of this Belshazzar's feast for the architriclino-basochien register was duly drawn up, beginning, "Inter pocula aurea restauranti, qui vulgo dicitur Rupes Cancali." Every one can imagine the fine page now added to the Golden Book of jurisprudential festivals.

Godeschal disappeared after signing the report, leaving the eleven guests, stimulated by the old captain of the Imperial Guard, to the wines, toasts, and liqueurs of a dessert composed of choice and early fruits, in pyramids that rivalled the obelisk of Thebes. By half-past ten the little sub-clerk was in such a state that Georges packed him into a coach, paid his fare, and gave the address of his mother to the driver. The remaining ten, all as drunk as Pitt and Dundas, talked of going on foot along the boulevards, considering the fine evening, to the house of the Marquise de las Florentinas y Cabirolos, where, about midnight, they might expect to find the most brilliant society of Paris. They felt the need of breathing the pure air into their lungs; but, with the exception of Georges, Giroudeau, du Bruel, and Finot, all four accustomed to Parisian orgies, not one of the party could walk. Consequently, Georges sent to a livery-stable for three open carriages, in which he drove his company for an hour round the exterior boulevards from Monmartre to the Barriere du Trone. They returned by Bercy, the quays, and the boulevards to the rue de Vendome.

The clerks were fluttering still in the skies of fancy to which youth is lifted by intoxication, when their amphitryon introduced them into Florentine's salon. There sparkled a bevy of stage princesses, who, having been informed, no doubt, of Frederic's joke, were amusing themselves by imitating the women of good society. They were then engaged in eating ices. The wax-candles flamed in the candelabra. Tullia's footmen and those of Madame du Val-Noble and Florine, all in full livery, where serving the dainties on silver salvers. The hangings, a marvel of Lyonnaise workmanship, fastened by gold cords, dazzled all eyes. The flowers of the carpet were like a garden. The richest "bibelots" and curiosities danced before the eyes of the new-comers.

At first, and in the state to which Georges had brought them, the clerks, and more particularly Oscar, believed in the Marquise de las Florentinas y Cabirolos. Gold glittered on four card-tables in the bed-chamber. In the salon, the women were playing at vingt-et-un, kept by Nathan, the celebrated author.

After wandering, tipsy and half asleep, through the dark exterior boulevards, the clerks now felt that they had wakened in the palace of Armida. Oscar, presented to the marquise by Georges, was quite stupefied, and did not recognize the danseuse he had seen at the Gaiete, in this lady, aristocratically decolletee and swathed in laces, till she looked like the vignette of a keepsake, who received him with manners and graces the like of which was neither in the memory nor the imagination of a young clerk rigidly brought up. After admiring the splendors of the apartment and the beautiful women there displayed, who had all outdone each other in their dress for this occasion, Oscar was taken by the hand and led by Florentine to a vingt-et-un table.

"Let me present you," she said, "to the beautiful Marquise d'Anglade, one of my nearest friends."

And she took Oscar to the pretty Fanny Beaupre, who had just made herself a reputation at the Porte-Saint-Martin, in a melodrama entitled "La Famille d'Anglade."

"My dear," said Florentine, "allow me to present to you a charming youth, whom you can take as a partner in the game."

"Ah! that will be delightful," replied the actress, smiling, as she looked at Oscar. "I am losing. Shall we go shares, monsieur?"

"Madame la marquise, I am at your orders," said Oscar, sitting down beside her.

"Put down the money; I'll play; you shall being me luck! See, here are my last hundred francs."

160

And the "marquise" took out from her purse, the rings of which were adorned with diamonds, five gold pieces. Oscar pulled out his hundred in silver five-franc pieces, much ashamed at having to mingle such ignoble coins with gold. In ten throws the actress lost the two hundred francs.

"Oh! how stupid!" she cried. "I'm banker now. But we'll play together still, won't we?"

Fanny Beaupre rose to take her place as banker, and Oscar, finding himself observed by the whole table, dared not retire on the ground that he had no money. Speech failed him, and his tongue clove to the roof of his mouth.

"Lend me five hundred francs," said the actress to the danseuse.

Florentine brought the money, which she obtained from Georges, who had just passed eight times at ecarte.

"Nathan has won twelve hundred francs," said the actress to Oscar. "Bankers always win; we won't let them fool us, will we?" she whispered in his ear.

Persons of nerve, imagination, and dash will understand how it was that poor Oscar opened his pocket-book and took out the note of five hundred francs which Desroches had given him. He looked at Nathan, the distinguished author, who now began, with Florine, to play a heavy game against the bank.

"Come, my little man, take 'em up," cried Fanny Beaupre, signing to Oscar to rake in the two hundred francs which Nathan and Florine had punted.

The actress did not spare taunts or jests on those who lost. She enlivened the game with jokes which Oscar thought singular; but reflection was stifled by joy; for the first two throws produced a gain of two thousand francs. Oscar then thought of feigning illness and making his escape, leaving his partner behind him; but "honor" kept him there. Three more turns and the gains were lost. Oscar felt a cold sweat running down his back, and he was sobered completely.

The next two throws carried off the thousand francs of their mutual stake. Oscar was consumed with thirst, and drank three glasses of iced punch one after the other. The actress now led him into the bed-chamber, where the rest of the company were playing, talking frivolities with an easy air. But by this time the sense of his wrong-doing overcame him; the figure of Desroches appeared to him like a vision. He turned aside to a dark corner and sat down, putting his handkerchief to his eyes, and wept. Florentine noticed the attitude of true grief, which, because it is sincere, is certain to strike the eye of one who acts. She ran to him, took the handkerchief from his hand, and saw his tears; then she led him into a boudoir alone.

"What is it, my child?" she said.

At the tone and accent of that voice Oscar recognized a motherly kindness which is often found in women of her kind, and he answered openly:—

"I have lost five hundred francs which my employer gave me to obtain a document to-morrow morning; there's nothing for me but to fling myself into the river; I am dishonored."

"How silly you are!" she said. "Stay where you are; I'll get you a thousand francs and you can win back what you've lost; but don't risk more than five hundred, so that you may be sure of your master's money. Georges plays a fine game at ecarte; bet on him."

Oscar, frightened by his position, accepted the offer of the mistress of the house.

"Ah!" he thought, "it is only women of rank who are capable of such kindness. Beautiful, noble, rich! how lucky Georges is!"

He received the thousand francs from Florentine and returned to bet on his hoaxer. Georges had just passed for the fourth time when Oscar sat down beside him. The other players saw with satisfaction the arrival of a new better; for all, with the instinct of gamblers, took the side of Giroudeau, the old officer of the Empire.

"Messieurs," said Georges, "you'll be punished for deserting me; I feel in the vein. Come, Oscar, we'll make an end of them!"

Georges and his partner lost five games running. After losing the thousand francs Oscar was seized with the fury of play and insisted on taking the cards himself. By the result of a chance not at all uncommon with those who play for the first time, he won. But Georges bewildered him with advice; told him when to throw the cards, and even snatched them from his hand; so that this conflict of wills and intuitions injured his vein. By three o'clock in the morning, after various changes of fortune, and still drinking punch, Oscar came down to his last hundred francs. He rose with a heavy head, completely stupefied, took a few steps forward, and fell upon a sofa in the boudoir, his eyes closing in a leaden sleep.

"Mariette," said Fanny Beaupre to Godeschal's sister, who had come in about two o'clock, "do you dine here to-morrow? Camusot and Pere Cardot are coming, and we'll have some fun."

"What!" cried Florentine, "and my old fellow never told me!"

"He said he'd tell you to-morrow morning," remarked Fanny Beaupre.

"The devil take him and his orgies!" exclaimed Florentine. "He and Camusot are worse than magistrates or stage-managers. But we have very good dinners here, Mariette," she continued. "Cardot always orders them from Chevet's; bring your Duc de Maufrigneuse and we'll make them dance like Tritons."

Hearing the names of Cardot and Camusot, Oscar made an effort to throw off his sleep; but he could only mutter a few words which were not understood, and then he fell back upon the silken cushions.

"You'll have to keep him here all night," said Fanny Beaupre, laughing, to Florentine.

"Oh! poor boy! he is drunk with punch and despair both. It is the second clerk in your brother's office," she said to Mariette. "He has lost the money his master gave him for some legal affair. He wanted to drown himself; so I lent him a thousand francs, but those brigands Finot and Giroudeau won them from him. Poor innocent!"

"But we ought to wake him," said Mariette. "My brother won't make light of it, nor his master either."

"Oh, wake him if you can, and carry him off with you!" said Florentine, returning to the salon to receive the adieux of some departing guests.

Presently those who remained began what was called "character dancing," and by the time it was broad daylight, Florentine, tired out, went to bed, oblivious to Oscar, who was still in the boudoir sound asleep.

# CHAPTER X

## ANOTHER CATASTROPHE

About eleven the next morning, a terrible sound awoke the unfortunate clerk. Recognizing the voice of his uncle Cardot, he thought it wise to feign sleep, and so turned his face into the yellow velvet cushions on which he had passed the night.

"Really, my little Florentine," said the old gentleman, "this is neither right nor sensible; you danced last evening in 'Les Ruines,' and you have spent the night in an orgy. That's deliberately going to work to lose your freshness. Besides which, it was ungrateful to inaugurate this beautiful apartment without even letting me know. Who knows what has been going on here?"

"Old monster!" cried Florentine, "haven't you a key that lets you in at all hours? My ball lasted till five in the morning, and you have the cruelty to come and wake me up at eleven!"

"Half-past eleven, Titine," observed Cardot, humbly. "I came out early to order a dinner fit for an archbishop at Chevet's. Just see how the carpets are stained! What sort of people did you have here?"

"You needn't complain, for Fanny Beaupre told me you were coming to dinner with Camusot, and to please you I've invited Tullia, du Bruel, Mariette, the Duc de Maufrigneuse, Florine, and Nathan. So you'll have the four loveliest creatures ever seen behind the foot-lights; we'll dance you a 'pas de Zephire.'"

"It is enough to kill you to lead such a life!" cried old Cardot; "and look at the broken glasses! What pillage! The antechamber actually makes me shudder—"

At this instant the wrathful old gentleman stopped short as if magnetized, like a bird which a snake is charming. He saw the outline of a form in a black coat through the door of the boudoir.

"Ah, Mademoiselle Cabirolle!" he said at last.

"Well, what?" she asked.

The eyes of the danseuse followed those of the little old man; and when she recognized the presence of the clerk she went off into such fits of laughter that not only was the old gentleman nonplussed, but Oscar was compelled to appear; for Florentine took him by the arm, still pealing with laughter at the conscience-stricken faces of the uncle and nephew.

"You here, nephew?"

"Nephew! so he's your nephew?" cried Florentine, with another burst of laughter. "You never told me about him. Why didn't Mariette carry you off?" she said to Oscar, who stood there petrified. "What can he do now, poor boy?"

"Whatever he pleases!" said Cardot, sharply, marching to the door as if to go away.

"One moment, papa Cardot. You will be so good as to get your nephew out of a scrape into which I led him; for he played the money of his master and lost it, and I lend him a thousand francs to win it back, and he lost that too."

"Miserable boy! you lost fifteen hundred francs at play at your age?"

"Oh, uncle, uncle!" cried poor Oscar, plunged by these words into all the horrors of his position, and falling on his knees before his uncle, with clasped hands, "It is twelve o'clock! I am lost, dishonored! Monsieur Desroches will have no pity! He gave me the money for an important affair, in which his pride was concerned. I was to get a paper at the Palais in the case of Vandernesse versus Vandernesse! What will become of me? Oh, save me for the sake of my father and aunt! Come with me to Monsieur Desroches, and explain it to him; make some excuse,—anything!"

These sentences were jerked out through sobs and tears that might have moved the sphinx of Luxor.

"Old skinflint!" said the danseuse, who was crying, "will you let your own nephew be dishonored,—the son of the man to whom you owe your fortune?—for his name is Oscar Husson. Save him, or Titine will deny you forever!"

"But how did he come here?" asked Cardot.

"Don't you see that the reason he forgot to go for those papers was because he was drunk and overslept himself. Georges and his cousin Frederic took all the clerks in his office to a feast at the Rocher de Cancale."

Pere Cardot looked at Florentine and hesitated.

"Come, come," she said, "you old monkey, shouldn't I have hid him better if there had been anything else in it?"

"There, take your five hundred francs, you scamp!" said Cardot to his nephew, "and remember, that's the last penny you'll ever get from me. Go and make it up with your master if you can. I'll return the thousand francs which you borrowed of mademoiselle; but I'll never hear another word about you."

Oscar disappeared, not wishing to hear more. Once in the street, however, he knew not where to go.

Chance which destroys men and chance which saves them were both making equal efforts for and against Oscar during that fateful morning. But he was doomed to fall before a master who forgave no failure in any affair he had once undertaken. When Mariette reached home that night, she felt alarmed at what might happen to the youth in whom her brother took interest and she wrote a hasty note to Godeschal, telling him what had happened to Oscar and inclosing a bank bill for five hundred francs to repair his loss. The kind-hearted creature went to sleep after charging her maid to carry the little note to Desroches' office before seven o'clock in the morning. Godeschal, on his side, getting up at six and finding that Oscar had not returned, guessed what had happened. He took the five hundred francs from his own little hoard and rushed to the Palais, where he obtained a copy of the judgment and returned in time to lay it before Desroches by eight o'clock.

Meantime Desroches, who always rose at four, was in his office by seven. Mariette's maid, not finding the brother of her mistress in his bedroom, came down to the office and there met Desroches, to whom she very naturally offered the note.

"Is it about business?" he said; "I am Monsieur Desroches."

"You can see, monsieur," replied the maid.

Desroches opened the letter and read it. Finding the five-hundred-franc note, he went into his private office furiously angry with his second clerk. About half-past seven he heard Godeschal dictating to the second head-clerk a copy of the document in question, and a few moments later the good fellow entered his master's office with an air of triumph in his heart.

"Did Oscar Husson fetch the paper this morning from Simon?" inquired Desroches.

"Yes, monsieur."

"Who gave him the money?"

"Why, you did, Saturday," replied Godeschal.

"Then it rains five-hundred-franc notes," cried Desroches. "Look here, Godeschal, you are a fine fellow, but that little Husson does not deserve such generosity. I hate idiots, but I hate still more the men who will go wrong in spite of the fatherly care which watches over them." He gave Godeschal Mariette's letter and the five-hundred-franc note which she had sent. "You must excuse my having opened it," he said, "but your sister's maid told me it was on business. Dismiss Husson."

"Poor unhappy boy! what grief he has caused me!" said Godeschal, "that tall ne'er-do-well of a Georges Marest is his evil genius; he ought to flee him like the plague; if not, he'll bring him to some third disgrace."

"What do you mean by that?" asked Desroches.

Godeschal then related briefly the affair of the journey to Presles.

"Ah! yes," said the lawyer, "I remember Joseph Bridau told me that story about the time it happened. It is to that meeting that we owe the favor Monsieur de Serizy has since shown in the matter of Joseph's brother, Philippe Bridau."

At this moment Moreau, to whom the case of the Vandernesse estate was of much importance, entered the office. The marquis wished to sell the land in parcels and the count was opposed to such a sale. The land-agent received therefore the first fire of Desroches' wrath against his ex-second clerk and all the threatening prophecies which he fulminated against him. The result was that this most sincere friend and protector of the unhappy youth came to the conclusion that his vanity was incorrigible.

"Make him a barrister," said Desroches. "He has only his last examination to pass. In that line, his defects might prove virtues, for self-love and vanity give tongues to half the attorneys."

At this time Clapart, who was ill, was being nursed by his wife,—a painful task, a duty without reward. The sick man tormented the poor creature, who was now doomed to learn what venomous and spiteful teasing a half-imbecile man, whom poverty had rendered craftily savage, could be capable of in the weary tete-a-tete of each endless day. Delighted to turn a sharpened arrow in the sensitive heart of the mother, he had, in a measure, studied the fears that Oscar's behavior and defects inspired in the poor woman. When a mother receives from her child a shock like that of the affair at Presles, she continues in a state of constant fear, and, by the manner in which his wife boasted of Oscar every time he obtained the slightest success, Clapart knew the extent of her secret uneasiness, and he took pains to rouse it on every occasion.

"Well, Madame," Clapart would say, "Oscar is doing better than I even hoped. That journey to Presles was only a heedlessness of youth. Where can you find young lads who do not commit just such faults?

Poor child! he bears his privations heroically! If his father had lived, he would never have had any. God grant he may know how to control his passions!" etc., etc.

While all these catastrophes were happening in the rue de Vendome and the rue de Bethisy, Clapart, sitting in the chimney corner, wrapped in an old dressing-gown, watched his wife, who was engaged over the fire in their bedroom in simultaneously making the family broth, Clapart's "tisane," and her own breakfast.

"Mon Dieu! I wish I knew how the affair of yesterday ended. Oscar was to breakfast at the Rocher de Cancale and spend the evening with a marquise—"

"Don't trouble yourself! Sooner or later you'll find out about your swan," said her husband. "Do you really believe in that marquise? Pooh! A young man who has senses and a taste for extravagance like Oscar can find such ladies as that on every bush—if he pays for them. Some fine morning you'll find yourself with a load of debt on your back."

"You are always trying to put me in despair!" cried Madame Clapart. "You complained that my son lived on your salary, and never has he cost you a penny. For two years you haven't had the slightest cause of complaint against him; here he is second clerk, his uncle and Monsieur Moreau pay all expenses, and he earns, himself, a salary of eight hundred francs. If we have bread to eat in our old age we may owe it all to that dear boy. You are really too unjust—"

"You call my foresight unjust, do you?" replied the invalid, crossly.

Just then the bell rang loudly. Madame Clapart ran to open the door, and remained in the outer room with Moreau, who had come to soften the blow which Oscar's new folly would deal to the heart of his poor mother.

"What! he gambled with the money of the office?" she cried, bursting into tears.

"Didn't I tell you so, hey?" said Clapart, appearing like a spectre at the door of the salon whither his curiosity had brought him.

"Oh! what shall we do with him?" said Madame Clapart, whose grief made her impervious to Clapart's taunt.

"If he bore my name," replied Moreau, "I should wait composedly till he draws for the conscription, and if he gets a fatal number I should not provide him with a substitute. This is the second time your son has committed a folly out of sheer vanity. Well, vanity may inspire fine deeds in war and may advance him in the career of a soldier. Besides, six years of military service will put some lead into his head; and as he has only his last legal examination to pass, it won't be much ill-luck for him if he doesn't become a lawyer till he is twenty-six; that is, if he wants to continue in the law after paying, as they say, his tax of blood. By that time, at any rate, he will have been severely punished, he will have learned experience, and contracted habits of subordination. Before making his probation at the bar he will have gone through his probations in life."

"If that is your decision for a son," said Madame Clapart, "I see that the heart of a father is not like that of a mother. My poor Oscar a common soldier!—"

"Would you rather he flung himself headforemost into the Seine after committing a dishonorable action? He cannot now become a solicitor; do you think him steady and wise enough to be a barrister? No. While his reason is maturing, what will he become? A dissipated fellow. The discipline of the army will, at least, preserve him from that."

"Could he not go into some other office? His uncle Cardot has promised to pay for his substitute; Oscar is to dedicate his graduating thesis to him."

At this moment carriage-wheels were heard, and a hackney-coach containing Oscar and all his worldly belongings stopped before the door. The luckless young man came up at once.

"Ah! here you are, Monsieur Joli-Coeur!" cried Clapart.

Oscar kissed his mother, and held out to Moreau a hand which the latter refused to take. To this rebuff Oscar replied by a reproachful look, the boldness of which he had never shown before. Then he turned on Clapart.

"Listen to me, monsieur," said the youth, transformed into a man. "You worry my poor mother devilishly, and that's your right, for she is, unfortunately, your wife. But as for me, it is another thing. I shall be of age in a few months; and you have no rights over me even as a minor. I have never asked anything of you. Thanks to Monsieur Moreau, I have never cost you one penny, and I owe you no gratitude. Therefore, I say, let me alone!"

Clapart, hearing this apostrophe, slunk back to his sofa in the chimney corner. The reasoning and the inward fury of the young man, who had just received a lecture from his friend Godeschal, silenced the imbecile mind of the sick man.

"A momentary temptation, such as you yourself would have yielded to at my age," said Oscar to Moreau, "has made me commit a fault which Desroches thinks serious, though it is only a peccadillo. I am more provoked with myself for taking Florentine of the Gaiete for a marquise than I am for losing fifteen hundred francs after a little debauch in which everybody, even Godeschal, was half-seas over. This time, at any rate, I've hurt no one by myself. I'm cured of such things forever. If you are willing to help me, Monsieur Moreau, I swear to you that the six years I must still stay a clerk before I can get a practice shall be spent without—"

"Stop there!" said Moreau. "I have three children, and I can make no promises."

"Never mind, never mind," said Madame Clapart to her son, casting a reproachful glance at Moreau. "Your uncle Cardot—"

"I have no longer an uncle Cardot," replied Oscar, who related the scene at the rue de Vendome.

Madame Clapart, feeling her legs give way under the weight of her body, staggered to a chair in the dining-room, where she fell as if struck by lightning.

"All the miseries together!" she said, as she fainted.

Moreau took the poor mother in his arms, and carried her to the bed in her chamber. Oscar remained motionless, as if crushed.

"There is nothing left for you," said Moreau, coming back to him, "but to make yourself a soldier. That idiot of a Clapart looks to me as though he couldn't live three months, and then your mother will be without a penny. Ought I not, therefore, to reserve for her the little money I am able to give? It was impossible to tell you this before her. As a soldier, you'll eat plain bread and reflect on life such as it is to those who are born into it without fortune."

"I may get a lucky number," said Oscar.

"Suppose you do, what then? Your mother has well fulfilled her duty towards you. She gave you an education; she placed you on the right road, and secured you a career. You have left it. Now, what can you do? Without money, nothing; as you know by this time. You are not a man who can begin a new career by taking off your coat and going to work in your shirt-sleeves with the tools of an artisan. Besides, your mother loves you, and she would die to see you come to that."

Oscar sat down and no longer restrained his tears, which flowed copiously. At last he understood this language, so completely unintelligible to him ever since his first fault.

"Men without means ought to be perfect," added Moreau, not suspecting the profundity of that cruel sentence.

"My fate will soon be decided," said Oscar. "I draw my number the day after to-morrow. Between now and then I will decide upon my future."

Moreau, deeply distressed in spite of his stern bearing, left the household in the rue de la Cerisaie to its despair.

Three days later Oscar drew the number twenty-seven. In the interests of the poor lad the former steward of Presles had the courage to go to the Comte de Serizy and ask for his influence to get Oscar into the cavalry. It happened that the count's son, having left the Ecole Polytechnique rather low in his class, was appointed, as a favor, sub-lieutenant in a regiment of cavalry commanded by the Duc de Maufrigneuse. Oscar had, therefore, in his great misfortune, the small luck of being, at the Comte de Serizy's instigation, drafted into that noble regiment, with the promise of promotion to quartermaster within a year. Chance had thus placed the ex-clerk under the command of the son of the Comte de Serizy.

Madame Clapart, after languishing for some days, so keenly was she affected by these catastrophes, became a victim to the remorse which seizes upon many a mother whose conduct has been frail in her youth, and who, in her old age, turns to repentance. She now considered herself under a curse. She attributed the sorrows of her second marriage and the misfortunes of her son to a just retribution by which God was compelling her to expiate the errors and pleasures of her youth. This opinion soon became a certainty in her mind. The poor woman went, for the first time in forty years, to confess herself to the Abbe Gaudron, vicar of Saint-Paul's, who led her into the practice of devotion. But so ill-used and loving a soul as that of Madame Clapart's could never be anything but simply pious. The Aspasia of the Directory wanted to expiate her sins in order to draw down the blessing of God on the head of her poor Oscar, and she henceforth vowed herself to works and deeds of the purest piety. She believed she had won the attention of heaven when she saved the life of Monsieur Clapart, who, thanks to her devotion, lived on to torture her; but she chose to see, in the tyranny of that imbecile mind, a trial inflicted by the hand of one who loveth while he chasteneth.

Oscar, meantime, behaved so well that in 1830 he was first sergeant of the company of the Vicomte de Serizy, which gave him the rank of sub-lieutenant of the line. Oscar Husson was by that time twenty-five years old. As the Royal Guard, to which his regiment was attached, was always in garrison in Paris, or within a circumference of thirty miles around the capital, he came to see his mother from time to time, and tell her his griefs; for he had the sense to see that he could never become an officer as matters then were. At that time the cavalry grades were all being taken up by the younger sons of noble families, and men without the article to their names found promotion difficult. Oscar's sole ambition was to leave the Guards and be appointed sub-lieutenant in a regiment of the cavalry of the line. In the month of February, 1830, Madame Clapart obtained this promotion for her son through the influence of Madame la Dauphine, granted to the Abbe Gaudron, now rector of Saint-Pauls.

Although Oscar outwardly professed to be devoted to the Bourbons, in the depths of his heart he was a liberal. Therefore, in the struggle of 1830, he went over to the side of the people. This desertion, which had an importance due to the crisis in which it took place, brought him before the eyes of the public. During the excitement of triumph in the month of August he was promoted lieutenant, received the cross of the Legion of honor, and was attached as aide-de-camp to La Fayette, who gave him the rank of captain in 1832. When the amateur of the best of all possible republics was removed from the command of the National guard, Oscar Husson, whose devotion to the new dynasty amounted to fanaticism, was appointed major of a regiment sent to Africa at the time of the first expedition undertaken by the Prince-royal. The Vicomte de Serizy chanced to be the lieutenant-colonel of this regiment. At the affair of the Makta, where the field had to be abandoned to the Arabs, Monsieur de Serizy was left wounded under a dead horse. Oscar, discovering this, called out to the squadron:

"Messieurs, it is going to death, but we cannot abandon our colonel."

He dashed upon the enemy, and his electrified soldiers followed him. The Arabs, in their first astonishment at this furious and unlooked-for return, allowed Oscar to seize the viscount, whom he flung across his horse, and carried off at full gallop,—receiving, as he did so, two slashes from yataghans on his left arm.

Oscar's conduct on this occasion was rewarded with the officer's cross of the Legion of honor, and by his promotion to the rank of lieutenant-colonel. He took the most affectionate care of the Vicomte de Serizy, whose mother came to meet him on the arrival of the regiment at Toulon, where, as we know, the young man died of his wounds.

The Comtesse de Serizy had not separated her son from the man who had shown him such devotion. Oscar himself was so seriously wounded that the surgeons whom the countess had brought with her from Paris thought best to amputate his left arm.

Thus the Comte de Serizy was led not only to forgive Oscar for his painful remarks on the journey to Presles, but to feel himself his debtor on behalf of his son, now buried in the chapel of the chateau de Serizy.

# CHAPTER XI

## OSCAR'S LAST BLUNDER

Some years after the affair at Makta, an old lady, dressed in black, leaning on the arm of a man about thirty-four years of age, in whom observers would recognize a retired officer, from the loss of an arm and the rosette of the Legion of honor in his button-hole, was standing, at eight o'clock, one morning in the month of May, under the porte-cochere of the Lion d'Argent, rue de Faubourg Saint-Denis, waiting, apparently, for the departure of a diligence. Undoubtedly Pierrotin, the master of the line of coaches running through the valley of the Oise (despatching one through Saint-Leu-Taverny and Isle-Adam to Beaumont), would scarcely have recognized in this bronzed and maimed officer the little Oscar Husson he had formerly taken to Presles. Madame Husson, at last a widow, was as little recognizable as her son. Clapart, a victim of Fieschi's machine, had served his wife better by death than by all his previous life. The idle lounger was hanging about, as usual, on the boulevard du Temple, gazing at the show, when the explosion came. The poor widow was put upon the pension list, made expressly for the families of the victim, at fifteen hundred francs a year.

The coach, to which were harnessed four iron-gray horses that would have done honor to the Messageries-royales, was divided into three compartments, coupe, interieur, and rotonde, with an imperiale above. It resembled those diligences called "Gondoles," which now ply, in rivalry with the railroad, between Paris and Versailles. Both solid and light, well-painted and well-kept, lined with fine blue cloth, and furnished with blinds of a Moorish pattern and cushions of red morocco, the "Swallow of the Oise" could carry, comfortably, nineteen passengers. Pierrotin, now about fifty-six years old, was little changed. Still dressed in a blue blouse, beneath which he wore a black suit, he smoked his pipe, and superintended the two porters in livery, who were stowing away the luggage in the great imperiale.

"Are your places taken?" he said to Madame Clapart and Oscar, eyeing them like a man who is trying to recall a likeness to his memory.

"Yes, two places for the interieur in the name of my servant, Bellejambe," replied Oscar; "he must have taken them last evening."

"Ah! monsieur is the new collector of Beaumont," said Pierrotin. "You take the place of Monsieur Margueron's nephew?"

"Yes," replied Oscar, pressing the arm of his mother, who was about to speak.

The officer wished to remain unknown for a time.

Just then Oscar thrilled at hearing the well-remembered voice of Georges Marest calling out from the street: "Pierrotin, have you one seat left?"

"It seems to me you could say 'monsieur' without cracking your throat," replied the master of the line of coaches of the Valley of the Oise, sharply.

Unless by the sound of the voice, Oscar could never have recognized the individual whose jokes had been so fatal to him. Georges, almost bald, retained only three or four tufts of hair above his ears; but these were elaborately frizzed out to conceal, as best they could, the nakedness of the skull. A fleshiness ill-placed, in other words, a pear-shaped stomach, altered the once elegant proportions of the ex-young man. Now almost ignoble in appearance and bearing, Georges exhibited the traces of disasters in love and a life of debauchery in his blotched skin and bloated, vinous features. The eyes had lost the brilliancy, the vivacity of youth which chaste or studious habits have the virtue to retain. Dressed like a man who is careless of his clothes, Georges wore a pair of shabby trousers, with straps intended for varnished boots; but his were of leather, thick-soled, ill-blacked, and of many months' wear. A faded waistcoat, a cravat, pretentiously tied, although the material was a worn-out foulard, bespoke the secret distress to which a former dandy sometimes falls a prey. Moreover, Georges appeared at this hour of the morning in an evening coat, instead of a surtout; a sure diagnostic of actual poverty. This coat, which had seen long service at balls, had now, like its master, passed from the opulent ease of former times to daily work. The seams of the black cloth showed whitening lines; the collar was greasy; long usage had frayed the edges of the sleeves into fringes.

And yet, Georges ventured to attract attention by yellow kid gloves, rather dirty, it is true, on the outside of which a signet ring defined a large dark spot. Round his cravat, which was slipped into a pretentious gold ring, was a chain of silk, representing hair, which, no doubt, held a watch. His hat, though worn rather jauntily, revealed, more than any of the above symptoms, the poverty of a man who was totally unable to pay sixteen francs to a hat-maker, being forced to live from hand to mouth. The former admirer of Florentine twirled a cane with a chased gold knob, which was horribly battered. The blue trousers, the waistcoat of a material called "Scotch stuff," a sky-blue cravat and a pink-striped cotton shirt, expressed, in the midst of all this ruin, such a latent desire to SHOW-OFF that the contrast was not only a sight to see, but a lesson to be learned.

"And that is Georges!" said Oscar, in his own mind,—"a man I left in possession of thirty thousand francs a year!"

"Has Monsieur *de* Pierrotin a place in the coupe?" asked Georges, ironically replying to Pierrotin's rebuff.

"No; my coupe is taken by a peer of France, the son-in-law of Monsieur Moreau, Monsieur le Baron de Canalis, his wife, and his mother-in-law. I have nothing left but one place in the interieur."

"The devil! so peers of France still travel in your coach, do they?" said Georges, remembering his adventure with the Comte de Serizy. "Well, I'll take that place in the interieur."

He cast a glance of examination on Oscar and his mother, but did not recognize them.

Oscar's skin was now bronzed by the sun of Africa; his moustache was very thick and his whiskers ample; the hollows in his cheeks and his strongly marked features were in keeping with his military bearing. The rosette of an officer of the Legion of honor, his missing arm, the strict propriety of his dress, would all have diverted Georges recollections of his former victim if he had had any. As for Madame Clapart, whom Georges had scarcely seen, ten years devoted to the exercise of the most severe piety had transformed her. No one would ever have imagined that that gray sister concealed the Aspasia of 1797.

An enormous old man, very simply dressed, though his clothes were good and substantial, in whom Oscar recognized Pere Leger, here came slowly and heavily along. He nodded familiarly to Pierrotin, who appeared by his manner to pay him the respect due in all lands to millionaires.

"Ha! ha! why, here's Pere Leger! more and more preponderant!" cried Georges.

"To whom have I the honor of speaking?" asked old Leger, curtly.

"What! you don't recognize Colonel Georges, the friend of Ali pacha? We travelled together once upon a time, in company with the Comte de Serizy."

One of the habitual follies of those who have fallen in the world is to recognize and desire the recognition of others.

"You are much changed," said the ex-farmer, now twice a millionaire.

"All things change," said Georges. "Look at the Lion d'Argent and Pierrotin's coach; they are not a bit like what they were fourteen years ago."

"Pierrotin now controls the whole service of the Valley of the Oise," replied Monsieur Leger, "and sends out five coaches. He is the bourgeois of Beaumont, where he keeps a hotel, at which all the diligences stop, and he has a wife and daughter who are not a bad help to him."

An old man of seventy here came out of the hotel and joined the group of travellers who were waiting to get into the coach.

"Come along, Papa Reybert," said Leger, "we are only waiting now for your great man."

"Here he comes," said the steward of Presles, pointing to Joseph Bridau.

Neither Georges nor Oscar recognized the illustrious artist, for his face had the worn and haggard lines that were now famous, and his bearing was that which is given by success. The ribbon of the Legion of honor adorned his black coat, and the rest of his dress, which was extremely elegant, seemed to denote an expedition to some rural fete.

At this moment a clerk, with a paper in his hand, came out of the office (which was now in the former kitchen of the Lion d'Argent), and stood before the empty coupe.

"Monsieur and Madame de Canalis, three places," he said. Then, moving to the door of the interieur, he named, consecutively, "Monsieur Bellejambe, two places; Monsieur de Reybert, three places; Monsieur— your name, if you please?" he said to Georges.

"Georges Marest," said the fallen man, in a low voice.

The clerk then moved to the rotunde, before which were grouped a number of nurses, country-people, and petty shopkeepers, who were bidding each other adieu. Then, after bundling in the six passengers, he called to four young men who mounted to the imperial; after which he cried: "Start!" Pierrotin got up beside his driver, a young man in a blouse, who called out: "Pull!" to his animals, and the vehicle, drawn by four horses brought at Roye, mounted the rise of the faubourg Saint-Denis at a slow trot.

But no sooner had it got above Saint-Laurent than it raced like a mail-cart to Saint-Denis, which it reached in forty minutes. No stop was made at the cheese-cake inn, and the coach took the road through the valley of Montmorency.

It was at the turn into this road that Georges broke the silence which the travellers had so far maintained while observing each other.

"We go a little faster than we did fifteen years ago, hey, Pere Leger?" he said, pulling out a silver watch.

"Persons are usually good enough to call me Monsieur Leger," said the millionaire.

"Why, here's our blagueur of the famous journey to Presles," cried Joseph Bridau. "Have you made any new campaigns in Asia, Africa, or America?"

"Sacrebleu! I've made the revolution of July, and that's enough for me, for it ruined me."

"Ah! you made the revolution of July!" cried the painter, laughing. "Well, I always said it never made itself."

"How people meet again!" said Monsieur Leger, turning to Monsieur de Reybert. "This, papa Reybert, is the clerk of the notary to whom you undoubtedly owe the stewardship of Presles."

"We lack Mistigris, now famous under his own name of Leon de Lora," said Joseph Bridau, "and the little young man who was stupid enough to talk to the count about those skin diseases which are now cured, and about his wife, whom he has recently left that he may die in peace."

"And the count himself, you lack him," said old Reybert.

"I'm afraid," said Joseph Bridau, sadly, "that the last journey the count will ever take will be from Presles to Isle-Adam, to be present at my marriage."

"He still drives about the park," said Reybert.

"Does his wife come to see him?" asked Leger.

"Once a month," replied Reybert. "She is never happy out of Paris. Last September she married her niece, Mademoiselle du Rouvre, on whom, since the death of her son, she spends all her affection, to a very rich young Pole, the Comte Laginski."

"To whom," asked Madame Clapart, "will Monsieur de Serizy's property go?"

"To his wife, who will bury him," replied Georges. "The countess is still fine-looking for a woman of fifty-four years of age. She is very elegant, and, at a little distance, gives one the illusion—"

"She will always be an illusion to you," said Leger, who seemed inclined to revenge himself on his former hoaxer.

"I respect her," said Georges. "But, by the bye, what became of that steward whom the count turned off?"

"Moreau?" said Leger; "why, he's the deputy from the Oise."

"Ha! the famous Centre man; Moreau de l'Oise?" cried Georges.

"Yes," returned Leger, "Moreau de l'Oise. He did more than you for the revolution of July, and he has since then bought the beautiful estate of Pointel, between Presles and Beaumont."

"Next to the count's," said Georges. "I call that very bad taste."

"Don't speak so loud," said Monsieur de Reybert, "for Madame Moreau and her daughter, the Baronne de Canalis, and the Baron himself, the former minister, are in the coupe."

"What 'dot' could he have given his daughter to induce our great orator to marry her?" said Georges.

"Something like two millions," replied old Leger.

"He always had a taste for millions," remarked Georges. "He began his pile surreptitiously at Presles—"

"Say nothing against Monsieur Moreau," cried Oscar, hastily. "You ought to have learned before now to hold your tongue in public conveyances."

Joseph Bridau looked at the one-armed officer for several seconds; then he said, smiling:—

"Monsieur is not an ambassador, but his rosette tells us he has made his way nobly; my brother and General Giroudeau have repeatedly named him in their reports."

"Oscar Husson!" cried Georges. "Faith! if it hadn't been for your voice I should never have known you."

"Ah! it was monsieur who so bravely rescued the Vicomte Jules de Serizy from the Arabs?" said Reybert, "and for whom the count has obtained the collectorship of Beaumont while awaiting that of Pontoise?"

"Yes, monsieur," said Oscar.

"I hope you will give me the pleasure, monsieur," said the great painter, "of being present at my marriage at Isle-Adam."

"Whom do you marry?" asked Oscar, after accepting the invitation.

"Mademoiselle Leger," replied Joseph Bridau, "the granddaughter of Monsieur de Reybert. Monsieur le comte was kind enough to arrange the marriage for me. As an artist I owe him a great deal, and he wished, before his death, to secure my future, about which I did not think, myself."

"Whom did Pere Leger marry?" asked Georges.

"My daughter," replied Monsieur de Reybert, "and without a 'dot.'"

"Ah!" said Georges, assuming a more respectful manner toward Monsieur Leger, "I am fortunate in having chosen this particular day to do the valley of the Oise. You can all be useful to me, gentlemen."

"How so?" asked Monsieur Leger.

"In this way," replied Georges. "I am employed by the 'Esperance,' a company just formed, the statutes of which have been approved by an ordinance of the King. This institution gives, at the end of ten years, dowries to young girls, annuities to old men; it pays the education of children, and takes charge, in short, of the fortunes of everybody."

"I can well believe it," said Pere Leger, smiling. "In a word, you are a runner for an insurance company."

"No, monsieur. I am the inspector-general; charged with the duty of establishing correspondents and appointing the agents of the company throughout France. I am only operating until the agents are selected; for it is a matter as delicate as it is difficult to find honest agents."

"But how did you lose your thirty thousand a year?" asked Oscar.

"As you lost your arm," replied the son of Czerni-Georges, curtly.

"Then you must have shared in some brilliant action," remarked Oscar, with a sarcasm not unmixed with bitterness.

"Parbleu! I've too many—shares! that's just what I wanted to sell."

By this time they had arrived at Saint-Leu-Taverny, where all the passengers got out while the coach changed horses. Oscar admired the liveliness which Pierrotin displayed in unhooking the traces from the whiffle-trees, while his driver cleared the reins from the leaders.

"Poor Pierrotin," thought he; "he has stuck like me,—not far advanced in the world. Georges has fallen low. All the others, thanks to speculation and to talent, have made their fortune. Do we breakfast here, Pierrotin?" he said, aloud, slapping that worthy on the shoulder.

"I am not the driver," said Pierrotin.

"What are you, then?" asked Colonel Husson.

"The proprietor," replied Pierrotin.

"Come, don't be vexed with an old acquaintance," said Oscar, motioning to his mother, but still retaining his patronizing manner. "Don't you recognize Madame Clapart?"

It was all the nobler of Oscar to present his mother to Pierrotin, because, at that moment, Madame Moreau de l'Oise, getting out of the coupe, overheard the name, and stared disdainfully at Oscar and his mother.

"My faith! madame," said Pierrotin, "I should never have known you; nor you, either, monsieur; the sun burns black in Africa, doesn't it?"

The species of pity which Oscar thus felt for Pierrotin was the last blunder that vanity ever led our hero to commit, and, like his other faults, it was punished, but very gently, thus:—

Two months after his official installation at Beaumont-sur-Oise, Oscar was paying his addresses to Mademoiselle Georgette Pierrotin, whose 'dot' amounted to one hundred and fifty thousand francs, and he married the pretty daughter of the proprietor of the stage-coaches of the Oise, toward the close of the winter of 1838.

The adventure of the journey to Presles was a lesson to Oscar Husson in discretion; his disaster at Florentine's card-party strengthened him in honesty and uprightness; the hardships of his military career taught him to understand the social hierarchy and to yield obedience to his lot. Becoming wise and capable, he was happy. The Comte de Serizy, before his death, obtained for him the collectorship at Pontoise. The influence of Monsieur Moreau de l'Oise and that of the Comtesse de Serizy and the Baron de Canalis secured, in after years, a receiver-generalship for Monsieur Husson, in whom the Camusot family now recognize a relation.

Oscar is a commonplace man, gentle, without assumption, modest, and always keeping, like his government, to a middle course. He excites neither envy nor contempt. In short, he is the modern bourgeois.

# ADDENDUM

The following personages appear in other stories of the Human Comedy.

Beaupre, Fanny
   Modest Mignon
   The Muse of the Department
   Scenes from a Courtesan's Life

Bridau, Joseph
   The Purse
   A Bachelor's Establishment
   A Distinguished Provincial at Paris
   Modeste Mignon
   Another Study of Woman
   Pierre Grassou
   Letters of Two Brides
   Cousin Betty
   The Member for Arcis

Bruel, Jean Francois du
   A Bachelor's Establishment
   The Government Clerks
   A Prince of Bohemia
   The Middle Classes

A Distinguished Provincial at Paris
A Daughter of Eve

Cabirolle, Madame
A Bachelor's Establishment

Cabirolle, Agathe-Florentine
Lost Illusions
A Distinguished Provincial at Paris
A Bachelor's Establishment

Canalis, Constant-Cyr-Melchior, Baron de
Letters of Two Brides
A Distinguished Provincial at Paris
Modeste Mignon
The Magic Skin
Another Study of Woman
Beatrix
The Unconscious Humorists
The Member for Arcis

Cardot, Jean-Jerome-Severin
Lost Illusions
A Distinguished Provincial at Paris
A Bachelor's Establishment
At the Sign of the Cat and Racket
Cesar Birotteau

Coralie, Mademoiselle
A Distinguished Provincial at Paris
A Bachelor's Establishment

Crottat, Alexandre
  Cesar Birotteau
  Colonel Chabert
  A Woman of Thirty
  Cousin Pons

Derville
  Gobseck
  The Gondreville Mystery
  Father Goriot
  Colonel Chabert
  Scenes from a Courtesan's Life

Desroches (son)
  A Bachelor's Establishment
  Colonel Chabert
  A Woman of Thirty
  The Commission in Lunacy
  The Government Clerks
  A Distinguished Provincial at Paris
  Scenes from a Courtesan's Life
  The Firm of Nucingen
  A Man of Business
  The Middle Classes

Finot, Andoche
  Cesar Birotteau
  A Bachelor's Establishment
  A Distinguished Provincial at Paris
  Scenes from a Courtesan's Life
  The Government Clerks

Grindot
  Cesar Birotteau
  Lost Illusions
  A Distinguished Provincial at Paris
  Scenes from a Courtesan's Life
  Beatrix
  The Middle Classes
  Cousin Betty

Lora, Leon de
  The Unconscious Humorists
  A Bachelor's Establishment
  Pierre Grassou
  Honorine
  Cousin Betty
  Beatrix

Loraux, Abbe
  A Bachelor's Establishment
  Cesar Birotteau
  Honorine

Lupin, Amaury
  The Peasantry

Marest, Frederic
  The Seamy Side of History
  The Member for Arcis

Marest, Georges
  The Peasantry

Maufrigneuse, Duc de
    The Secrets of a Princess
    A Bachelor's Establishment
    Scenes from a Courtesan's Life

Poiret, the elder
    The Government Clerks
    Father Goriot
    Scenes from a Courtesan's Life
    The Middle Classes

Rouvre, Marquis du
    The Imaginary Mistress
    Ursule Mirouet

Schinner, Hippolyte
    The Purse
    A Bachelor's Establishment
    Pierre Grassou
    Albert Savarus
    The Government Clerks
    Modeste Mignon
    The Imaginary Mistress
    The Unconscious Humorists

Serizy, Comte Hugret de
    A Bachelor's Establishment
    Honorine
    Modeste Mignon
    Scenes from a Courtesan's Life

Serizy, Comtesse de
    The Thirteen
    Ursule Mirouet
    A Woman of Thirty
    Scenes from a Courtesan's Life
    Another Study of Woman
    The Imaginary Mistress

Serizy, Vicomte de
    Modeste Mignon
    The Imaginary Mistress

Vandenesse, Marquis Charles de
    A Woman of Thirty
    A Daughter of Eve

Vandenesse, Comte Felix de
    The Lily of the Valley
    Lost Illusions
    A Distinguished Provincial at Paris
    Cesar Birotteau
    Letters of Two Brides
    The Marriage Settlement
    The Secrets of a Princess
    Another Study of Woman
    The Gondreville Mystery
    A Daughter of Eve

Printed in the USA
CPSIA information can be obtained
at www.ICGtesting.com
LVHW022147200823
755761LV00007B/1198